Walter Savage Landor, Alphonso Gerald Newcomer

Selections from the Imaginary conversations of Walter Savage

Landor

Walter Savage Landor, Alphonso Gerald Newcomer

Selections from the Imaginary conversations of Walter Savage Landor

ISBN/EAN: 9783337278595

Printed in Europe, USA, Canada, Australia, Japan

Cover: Foto ©Andreas Hilbeck / pixelio.de

More available books at **www.hansebooks.com**

SELECTIONS

FROM THE

IMAGINARY CONVERSATIONS

OF

WALTER SAVAGE LANDOR

EDITED, WITH NOTES AND AN INTRODUCTION

BY

ALPHONSO G. NEWCOMER

*Associate Professor of English in the Leland Stanford
Junior University*

NEW YORK

HENRY HOLT AND COMPANY

PREFACE.

THESE selections do not profess to be fairly representative of Landor's prose. The aim has been to include, not what is most characteristic, but what is most interesting and instructive, therefore most suitable for those who are beginning their studies in literature. For Landor must be approached with circumspection: some of his most characteristic work, delightful indeed as the recreation of mature and meditative years, has no place here. In the Introduction, however, an attempt has been made to restore the balance. But after all, and making the largest allowance for personal taste, no selection can differ very much from Mr. Colvin's. The fact is that of Landor's several thousand pages of prose, that which can make an appeal at once wide and deep can be gathered into the compass of a modest volume. The rest is like the vast plains of the Dakotas—fertile, but unpicturesque.

For the reassurance of those who still look askance at the *Imaginary Conversations*, let Mr. Colvin's opinion be cited, that to sound perpetually the praises of De Quincey's prose is to call away attention from the best to the second best—an opinion in which the present editor, with all admiration for De Quincey, entirely concurs. Not that Landor is to supplant, but only to supplement, De Quincey, Macaulay, Scott, and the rest, in a judicious course of English reading. Such a course must often begin with the second best—at least it must begin where interest is most readily engaged. But it must not be allowed to degenerate into a romantic debauch. And Landor's prose, one thinks, should afford precisely the right corrective, doubly needed at a time when the classic board is so frugally spread.

Such speculations, however, do not settle a question like this. Matthew Arnold was fond of pointing out that the value of any discipline is to be measured by its power of engaging the emotions and thereby exerting an influence upon the sense for conduct and the sense for beauty. By this test, applied and observed in the classroom, the *Imaginary Conversations* do not fail. Perhaps no element in literature awakens a livelier response than the dramatic, and in these dramatic dialogues the student is brought face to face with matters of enduring, interest. Humanity in its manifold aspects, with its clashes of opinion, its impulses to action, its gradations of character, is always in the foreground. There is no recital of facts to be committed to memory, and there are few flights of rhetoric to invite desultory discussion of words and sentences. But there is much that will demand original insight and call forth the highest powers of interpretation, while the style in its absolute purity teaches silently its own lesson.

The text of this edition is Mr. Crump's with corrections of manifest errors, which text is in turn Mr. Forster's with corrections and conventionalized spelling and punctuation.

A. G. N.

STANFORD UNIVERSITY, CAL.
April, 1899.

CONTENTS.

INTRODUCTION.

It can be no error of prejudgment to say that Landor has taken very nearly his final station among English men of letters. If that station is not in the circle of the consecrated it is yet very high among the elect, among those whose aims and achievements alike set them safely above the ranks of the merely great. Landor needs no apologist to-day. It may be that his title to fame has never been seriously questioned. But between immoderate self-praise and uncritical disparage-ment the title has sometimes been obscured. For this man had the insolence of genius as scarcely another since Pindar, and there have been not a few, from Byron down, who have derided that inso-lence unmercifully. On the other hand, it is not strange that some, under the spell of a personality so commanding and a voice so manifestly inspired, should set no bounds to their eulogy. But there have always been sober minds that knew how to steer the middle course. And the sober minds are now all that are left.

Still, the uniqueness of his position makes the task of criticism delicate and difficult. We can-not regard him as the prophet of any age, least of all his own. Neither a leader nor a disciple, he stands quite apart, and wherever the circle of his

horizon may lie, ours can only intersect it,—the two
will never coincide. We cannot apply to him the
larger criticism of relations and movements, of
which indeed he himself knew nothing. We escape
one task, but the standards of comparison which
facilitate and validate judgment escape us, leaving
us to measure him by himself alone. And he
would have wished it so. We know that the critic
who isolates his subject cuts his own clews. It is
what Landor did when he ventured upon criticism.
But when Landor becomes our subject, we have
the satisfaction of knowing that he isolated himself.
We can accept the responsibility and evade the
reproach.

At the worst we can fall back upon appreciation
and feel that when that is duly accorded our task
is done. There is not much to expound. Not that
Landor never preaches; he does so, quite too often
for the reader's peace of mind, and he doubtless intended some portions of his work to be distinctly
doctrinal. Only, we know better than to look for consistent doctrine from one whose logic was little more
than predilection. It would not be the part of wisdom then to dissect for truth. Yet truth has a way
of slipping out between inconsistencies, and the
debt of gratitude may as well be acknowledged.
Nor is truth the whole. In the presence of so con-
summate an art and so strong and individual an
artist, the most casual appraiser may not make
light of his task.

Walter Savage Landor was born in January, 1775,

and died in the autumn of 1864. The octogenarians of our literature, from Gower to Tennyson, we can almost count on our fingers. Nonagenarians were Izaak Walton, Thomas Hobbes, and Samuel Rogers. Landor came within four months of being named with the latter. We are not used to dealing with nonagenarians. To read of a man who died no longer ago than the close of our Civil War seeking for a publisher back in 1823 when Byron was setting forth on his fatal expedition to Greece, and then to be told that this man was nearly fifty years old at the time of the search puts us strangely out of our reckoning. The right perspective of life eludes us. Was this a young man seeking a publisher, or an old one? And who were his contemporaries? Macaulay? But Landor had published poetry and might have been accounted famous before Macaulay was born. Coleridge, then? But the young poet Swinburne went to Florence to receive the old poet's blessing half a life-time after Coleridge's death. Living to become the debtor for more than kindness of the Brownings in Italy, and the guest of the sculptor-poet Story, whose death was but recently recorded, he was yet, in his youth, with some disparity of years it is true, the friend of that Dr. Parr who could give vehement stamp for stamp in a heated argument with Dr. Johnson. He barely missed seeing Goldsmith. Time and distance dwindle as we look back through the overlapping lives of Landor, Johnson, Swift, Milton, Shakespeare.

It was a matter of some pride to him that he too

"drank of Avon, a dangerous draught." For he was born in the ancient town of Warwick, in Warwickshire, about eight miles above the spot that is linked forever with Shakespeare's name. Becoming, like his famous countryman, a poet and a dramatist, he exercised like him the poet's right to send his fancy roaming through forests of Arden that are doubtfully bounded by English shires. Yet we like to see, or to imagine we see, behind the love of trees and flowers that so pervades the man's written words something of the Warwickshire the child knew, the willow-hung banks of the placid Avon, the majestic elms and chestnut-woods, and the tall, luxuriant green hedge-rows stretching mile upon mile.

The life of the child, however, was hardly idyllic. The eldest son of well-conditioned parents, his education and the nature of it were foregone conclusions. At the age of four and a half he was sent away to school. Even upon the hardiest nature such early orphanage must work lasting injury, stunting the tender growths of sympathy, substituting for the restraints of love the restraints of authority, and leaving unlearned the joys of obedience and self-denial. There is at least some excuse for the perverse and haughty temper with which Landor grew up to manhood.

The records of his youth are not abundant. Mr. Forster, the friend of his latter years and his authorized biographer, did not meet him till he had passed sixty, when imagination was already beginning to make myths of reminiscences and reminiscences of myths. Of course his education was classical, of the old type so hard now to regard approvingly and yet productive of such wonderful results. Looked at through the recollections of its martyrs, it would seem to have been one endless task of writing Latin verses. And that accomplishment, genuine enough in Landor's case, for he is one of the very few who have succeeded in writing real poetry in a dead language, is in itself a barren thing. Yet when we read his *Hellenics* and hear

> through the trumpet of a child of Rome
> Ring the pure music of the flutes of Greece,

or when we learn from Mrs. Browning how he talked with her till "the ashes of antiquity burned again" in his hands, we are readier to listen with patience to the tales of how once the excellence of his Latin verses won for his schoolfellows a holiday, or how his later dismissal from Rugby was the result of his declining to correct the quantity of a Latin syllable when indeed no correction could be made.

After Rugby came a year and a half at Oxford. But a foolish prank and a more foolish denial of guilt made his further stay there impossible, and, not yet twenty, he went to face the world in London. The trite remark that well-learned lessons of humility and self-mastery are a better equipment for life than any inheritance of wealth or influence has seldom been so well illustrated. It is impossible to say that Landor succeeded in life.

His maintenance and social position were sufficiently secure from the first, though of course through no efforts of his own. His splendid intellectual and imaginative endowment made possible the literary achievements which establish his fame. But in prudence, tact, and all those delicate social adjustments and compromises that make for individual and collective happiness, his history presents a long series of failures, and he pathetically admitted as much in his old age. The details of his successive quarrels—with his father, his neighbors, his publishers, with civil authorities—need not be repeated here. The quarrels themselves are of no interest—many men before and since have quarreled; but where is the man who could solace himself afterward as this man did, by writing a lyric or a tragedy, or, should the whim so dictate, a Latin poem on the death of Ulysses?—betokening beneath the tempestuous surface what unsounded depths of calm!

He fell into the life that seemed ordained, the life of a man of letters and leisure, varied chiefly by his frequent changes of residence and friends. One or two episodes stand out. In 1808, when all England was stirred by Napoleon's aggressive designs upon Spain, he impulsively rushed off to Corunna and devoted to the cause of the rising Spaniards ten thousand reals and his personal services for three months at the head of a troop enrolled at his expense. That the enterprise came to little beyond an honorary colonel's commission which some years later, in a fit of indignation, was sent back to the restored King Ferdinand, cannot detract from the magnanimity of the spirit that prompted it. And poetry is the richer for it by the tragedy of *Count Julian.*

The same impulsiveness is revealed in the rather melodramatic story of his courtship. "By Heaven!" he exclaimed, as, entering a ballroom at Bath, he was smitten with the vision of a pretty face encircled with curls, "that's the nicest girl in the room, and I'll marry her." And within six weeks he made good his boast. The marriage was not a happy one. After twenty-four years of growing estrangement came a final separation. One might safely have prophesied as much of the man who could write Latin Alcaics against the Ministry during his honeymoon and inclose the verses, along with the announcement of his marriage, to his old Whig friend Parr. Still, it is only fair to add that Mrs. Landor once interrupted his reading of his own verses to watch a Punch performing on the street.

Apart from several years spent in South Wales, and at Llanthony Abbey in Monmouthshire, his English residence was chiefly at Bath. Twice he fled from unpleasantnesses of one kind or another to Italy, the retreat of so many English men of letters, where doubtless he consoled himself as he fancied Boccaccio consoled Petrarch: "There is, and ever will be, in all countries and under all governments, an ostracism for their greatest men." "Such men," writes Cleone to Aspasia, thinking how Pindar and Æschylus had exchanged Greece for

Sicily, "are under no dominion . . . We will reproach them for emigration, when we reproach a man for lying down in his neighbor's field, because the grass is softer in it than in his own." Besides, Florence had driven forth Dante and Petrarch in the past—in all humility now she might receive Landor. And at Florence and the neighboring town of Fiesole he spent many of his most peaceful and prolific years, weaving and wearing proudly his "exotic laurel." Thither admirers came from time to time to pay their tributes, and there he found one or two friends to solace his lonely age. There too, after nearly ninety years of tumultuous life, came death, likewise a friend. And there, in the English churchyard not far from the grave of Elizabeth Barrett Browning, whither she had preceded him by three years, he sleeps to-day.

These bare biographical facts but faintly reveal the character behind them. It is a character not easily understood, a strange combination of fierceness and tenderness, of restless energy and proud reserve. Perhaps few men have succeeded in uniting, in the same degree as Landor, the active and the contemplative life. It was a characteristic picture which he drew of himself at Llanthony Abbey, employing his mornings in cutting off the heads of the thistles with his stick and musing among the beautiful and peaceful tribes of the flowers. Characteristic, too, though perhaps apocryphal, is the story which Emerson and others have repeated after Milnes, that he once threw his

cook out of the window into a flower-bed, to exclaim
in immediate remorse, "Good God! I forgot the
violets." It was this nature that enabled him in boyhood to excel alike in boxing and in Latin, and in
manhood to produce through seventy turbulent years
a body of poetry and prose that for sustained
serenity stands quite without an equal.

Those who knew him well often likened him to a
lion, and we imagine the comparison was singularly
apt. The upright bearing, the proud poise of the
massive, firm-set head, the ruddy, prominent face,
with lifted eyebrows, large keen gray eyes, and
compressed lips drooping at the corners, the oft-
clenched hands, the full rich voice, and the resonant
crescendo laughter, were no less than leonine.
The external features are compatible too with
what we know of the inner nature—the vitality of
spirit that conquered one generation after another
of fearful but fascinated admirers, and the vigor of
intellect that, beyond eighty years, compelled Carlyle's half-incredulous cry, "The unsubduable old
Roman!" But the lion slept sometimes, and the
Roman sheathed his sword. "I found him noble
and courteous," wrote Emerson of him in 1833,
"living in a cloud of pictures at his villa Gherar-
descha . . . I had inferred from his books, or
magnified from some anecdotes, an impression of
Achillean wrath, . . . an untamable petulance, . . .
but certainly on this May day his courtesy veiled
that haughty mind, and he was the most patient
and gentle of hosts." "Chivalresque of the old
school" is Mr. Kirkup's phrase; and Miss Kate

Field relates how, as she one day picked up his glasses which he had accidentally dropped, he responded with instant wit and indescribable grace, "Ah, this is not the first time you have caught my eyes."

One would like to dwell upon the benignant side of his character. He took delight in the society of dogs and children, of beautiful girls and old men. He was fond of music, though perhaps chiefly for its associations—"Alas, how very few things *are* worth an old song?" His love of flowers amounted to a passion, but he liked to see the shaping hand of the artist among them, to find them in old, orderly gardens. He imported for planting thousands of cones of the cedars of Lebanon, as if old associations might be transplanted too. America, as the home of Washington and freedom, was attractive to his intellect, but it is doubtful whether the virgin wilderness could have held his heart. He preferred Italy with her history, her pictures, her cathedrals and saints. He was something of an Epicure after the old ideal—an ideal which embraced not a little that is Stoic. He was personally fastidious in the extreme, kept religiously from public dinners, preferring to dine alone in subdued light, cultivated the pleasures of the senses through abstemiousness, and by judicious alternation of physical activity with seasons of meditation and repose made life yield its richest enjoyments and turned age itself into a benign and mellowing influence.

But the melancholy record of his social failure

remains. His impetuous temper, his crotchets, his
prejudices, his unconquerable hatreds—of kings,
priests, Frenchmen—set him almost hopelessly out of
the society of his compeers. Modesty and humility
were never among his virtues. Of his personal and
intellectual gifts he had reason to be proud. But
reasonableness and consistency were also not among
his virtues. He knew the supreme worth of intellect and culture, he was a Whig and a republican, he professed to despise rank, and yet, like
De Quincey, though apparently with even less
warrant than De Quincey, he clung to the tradition
of a patrician descent and would have fought to
defend the memory of Sir Arnold Savage, a doubtful ancestor whose name he bore. At school he
never competed for a prize, and the reason is to be
found in the first line of that quatrain which has
become classic—

> I strove with none, for none was worth my strife.

And we read the same pride, unbroken still though
tempered with pathos, in those other lines of his
old age in which he bewails the fate that made
him outlive his friends—

> Who had so many—I could once count three.

Such an untamed, undisciplined, but august barbarian he remained to the end. With all his years,
his boasted philosophy, his familiar intercourse
with the wise men of antiquity, he cannot be said
to have attained the philosophic mind. He was a
man of splendid gifts who chose to be satisfied with

those gifts as he found them. He never thought of learning from another how he might improve them —perhaps he never had a suspicion that they could be improved. It was enough to feel that Nature and Heaven had nobly dowered him. "I am not inobservant of distinctions," he closes proudly a letter written in his dotage to the English ambassador at Florence,—"You by the favor of a minister are the Marquis of Normanby, I by the grace of God am WALTER SAVAGE LANDOR."

It was these things that proved so irritating to all whose tolerance could not be extended to another's intolerance. It was these things, too, coupled with a natural exclusiveness of spirit, that resulted in that lifelong semi-isolation which, while picturesque in its way, worked disastrously upon the man's whole moral and artistic product, distorting its perspective, chilling its fervor, and sapping its humanity. But the pride was so fearlessly paraded, the isolation so heroically endured, that in the eyes of us who look from a safe distance and through the tranquilizing medium of years the personality suffers but little. We yield to the fascination of the picture and turn from censure to admiration. After all, wrongheadedness is more tolerable than thickheadedness. He who errs through pride or passion may rouse our anger— he does not call down our contempt. We never pity him, which is very much to his advantage in the end. He has his foibles, we say, but, as Landor himself so tersely put it, *he has his foibles* is never said of a weak man. "Great men," admits Diogenes in the conversation between him and Plato, "too often have greater faults than little men can find room for." This great man had very many; but they are buried with him, while the great accomplishment stands.

And it will stand. There is little literary work of the present century of which one can speak with more confidence than of Landor's. For there is little work that rises so clear of its age and environment or is less exposed to the fallacy of personal and temporal estimates. He did not need to write for money; he was not oppressed with the burden of a message to be delivered to men. Fortune placed him far above the pack of hungry reviewers; temperament delivered him from the nightmare of social reform. Sometimes indignation made his verses. Sometimes, perhaps too often, as we have seen, he felt moved to speak out for the needs of the time as he conceived them, and he condescended to homily. But the Landor who will live for us is the Landor who took refuge from the clamor and confusion of a restless age amid the eternal verities of the human spirit and wrought their substance to the beauty of his art. And he wrought unmoved by base motives of profit or praise. He declared that he neither bid nor cared for any man's praise. If the profession of indifference ring not wholly sincere, if beneath his too boisterous contempt of the suffrages of the crowd we read a secret chafing over its neglect, something may be con-ceded to the hunger of human nature for recognition and reward.   The Homer of his *Idyls* confesses to

> A pardonable fault : we wish for listeners
> Whether we speak or sing : the young and old
> Alike are weak in this, wise and unwise.

But the certainty remains that Landor never abated one jot of his high ideals to conciliate any form of homage.

The high ideals must be conceded.   If literature did not grow out of the stress of his real life, it had yet his entire adoration. He worked with undisguised reverence for the work of his hands, and the stamp of the consecrated artist is on all he did.   His poetry perhaps reflects this quality best.   Before his twenty-third year, when the passion and exuberance of youth should be at their height, he wrote, in blank verse, and only by the merest chance in English instead of Latin, his heroic poem *Gebir*, on the theme of ambition, a marvel of concentration, classic finish, and lofty and chaste imagery.   He claimed no lesser poets than Pindar and Milton for his masters.   Such work was not for the multitude. It was not fervid and romantic enough, not sufficiently charged with emotion, color, and sound. And so with everything that followed.   Apart from several particularly striking or felicitous lines and passages of a character to be described below, his poetry has remained a sealed book to all but the few who are fitted by temperament and cultivation to appreciate it.   His one considerable drama, the tragedy of *Count Julian*, is carved as out of marble, with scarcely more human warmth or charm. Perhaps his peculiar poetic genius found its best expression in the severe *Hellenics* of his mature years.

Yet we must not overlook the countless fugitive little lyrics and epigrams that were produced, sometimes almost improvised, amid sterner labors, and that fairly rival in playful wit, tenderness, and pathos the works of the world's masters of personal and amatory verse from Anacreon and Catullus to André Chénier. Literature has nothing more exquisite and few things more rememberable than the eight lines in which the memory of Rose Aylmer is enshrined. Indeed, of Landor's poetry in general, epic, dramatic, or lyric, while it must be admitted that it misses the qualities of supreme greatness, it must also be said that it maintains a high level of excellence, and that some of it fairly attains perfection in its kind. To a passage like *The Death of Artemidora*, first printed in *Pericles and Aspasia*, it is idle to bring the scales.

Between Landor's poetry and his prose one hesitates to adjudge precedence. He bore the almost unique distinction of writing in the two modes with equal ease. No doubt his fame rests chiefly on his prose. Though narrower in range, it is larger in bulk, about as four to one, and this disparity, from so quintessential a pen, is real. Prose should prove a more native element, one thinks, to him who believed in a "gentle and regular and long fermentation" before composition. In prose, too, the touchstones are fewer, for the masters are few, and Landor takes his seat among them without dispute. The *Pericles and Aspasia* is one of those final achievements which criticism cannot touch. The surprise is that such pure imagination and flawless art should find an adequate medium in prose. We are taught a new reverence for this humble servant of our daily thoughts.

Three of these prose compositions rose to the dignity of " works." The *Citation and Examination of William Shakespeare* was the first and the least. The idea of portraying this universal genius in his immaturity, and under a disgrace with which Landor was quite too prone to sympathize, was audacious enough. But the execution failed. The piece gains less than might have been expected from the author's personal knowledge of the scene of the traditional deer-stealing, and it loses immeasurably by its theologizing and its heavy attempts at Elizabethan dialect and country-wit. *Pericles and Aspasia*, which followed, has already been mentioned. It is in the form of an epistolary correspondence throughout, and aims to restore to the imagination with some detail the golden age of Greece. It may not be the real Greek life that we get in its pages—we cannot know; but no true lover of that vanished vision will have it otherwise. Beyond the possibility of exaggeration at least the ancient glory must have been, to light up such reflections after two thousand years. It is something of a descent to the *Pentameron*, which came last. But here, too, Landor is a loving restorer of the antique. Boccaccio converses with Petrarch until mediæval

Tuscany lives again.   The appraisement of Dante by
the lesser poet, whether we name him Petrarch or
Landor, is narrow and disappointing, yet redeemed
by some things that must surely compel the forgiveness of the great Florentine's most jealous admirers.

Landor began his writings in prose, however,
with the work which is still most closely linked
with his memory, namely, those *Imaginary Conversations* that he poured so copiously through the press
between 1824 and 1829 and fitfully to the very end.
It was these that first wrung from the general
public a chary applause and firmly established the
name of the author, who was then already fifty
years old.   His longer prose pieces described
above followed most of them in time, and, as we
have seen, conformed to them in method with only
a slight variation in the case of *Pericles and Aspasia.*
This method, which constitutes his sole prose
method (though still with no narrow range), was
virtually a new one.   The dialogue as a literary
form is as old as Plato, indeed as old as the drama
or the epic, but the imaginary conversation between
great men or women of the past was impossible at
an early stage of history, and nothing of the kind
before Landor's, and scarcely anything since, has
met with any measure of success.   In the face of
Landor's success it seems foolish to hint that his
choice of method was not wholly wise.   But few
things that he did were wholly wise.   His parsimony
of phrase, his weak narrative talent, his gift for
description, his proneness to moralize, might well
have argued failure in so essentially dramatic a

thing as the ideal dialogue. And from the dramatic
standpoint he does often fail. But again he
succeeds by virtue of powers that overrode his
weaknesses. Supreme among these was the poet's
gift of imagination. The vision of past ages was
on his eyes, the voices of great men were in his
ears—of heroes, priests, poets, sages, kings. Even
when the great voices fail we have always one to
replace them—Landor's own. Sometimes the sub-
stitution strikes harsh or thin, but not often. The
poet seldom fails to rise to the level of whatever
greatness.

It is worth while to examine more closely the
method of these conversations, "so delightful to
read in, so hard to read through," and containing,
if we may trust Landor's own estimate, a body of
prose unequaled by a single author in two thousand
years. They number more than one hundred and
fifty and vary in length from two to ten or even
a hundred pages, making five or six weighty
volumes. Of this extensive and diverse material
there can be no final classification. In Mr.
Forster's edition there are five divisions: Classical
Dialogues (Greek and Roman), Dialogues of
Sovereigns and Statesmen, of Literary Men, of
Famous Women, and Miscellaneous Dialogues.
Mr. Colvin, considering more especially the nature
of their contents, would separate them into
Dramatic on the one hand and Reflective and
Discursive on the other. In the further discussion
of them here they will be considered in the two

major divisions of Philosophic and Dramatic and the two minor ones of Political and Critical.

The method of construction is the simplest of dialogue methods. Two characters, or sometimes more, from a chosen period of history or even from the writer's own circle of acquaintances not excluding himself, are brought together upon any or no pretext and discourse upon whatever subjects may be supposed to engage their interests. The discourse is not necessarily consecutive. In the longer dialogues, the speakers range freely from politics to poetry, from cathedrals to kitchens. A story even may be introduced, though seldom happily, for Landor's tales have not the charm of his beloved Boccaccio's. Sometimes there is a beautiful or majestic background, as when Epicurus walks with his girl pupils in his garden, or when Sir Philip Sidney invites Greville to a seat beneath his oak, but in general there is only the barest suggestion of scene, and the characters stand forth as nakedly as the actors on an ancient stage. Stage directions, of course, are not required, though hints of the action, as of the background, are sometimes to be found in the words of the interlocutors. The hints are not always so deftly given as to conceal their dramatic purpose, but life and picturesqueness are gained; as when Sergius is made to say, after a ribald jest, "Mahomet, thou art the heartiest laugher under heaven; prythee let thy beard cover thy throat again"; or as when Princess Mary expostulates with Elizabeth, "But why call me *Highness*, drawing back and losing half your stature in the circumference of the courtesy."

No fact needs more to be impressed upon one who would understand these conversations than that history constitutes for them only a point of departure. Landor's ends were literary, ethical, critical—anything but historical. The learning displayed is varied, but seldom profound. Profound insight he had, but profound scholarship he had not. He did not build so much upon patient investigation as upon wide reading and prolonged reflection. Many of the dialogues were composed aloud among the hills of Fiesole. Books once read were given away, and he cared to remember them only well enough to keep from repeating any part of their contents. His recollections were overlaid with additions of his imagination until there grew up a second history, or rather mythology, of his own. And of this mythology the conversations were made. Of course he generally preserved the historical background, and he did not disdain occasional allusions to familiar facts or traditions, as when we find Diogenes chaffing Plato over the affair of the plucked fowl, or Polycrates pursued by his discarded ring. But, jealously guarding his claim to the title of poet, of creative writer, he adhered rigidly to the plan of using no phrases historically recorded of his personages. An anachronism, too, was only a license,—remember the saving title *Imaginary,*—and gave him no more concern than it gave Shakespeare. "Poetry is not tied to chronology," he would say with scorn. And

so Bacon is made to seek consolation of Hooker,
who died twenty years before Bacon's fall, and
Machiavelli draws a lesson from the defeat of the
Spanish Armada! With such a purpose and method
it was inevitable that there should be some ideali-
zation. We may never assume that an historical
character was as great or as little as Landor por-
trays it. Yet an idealized portrait is sometimes
truer than a photograph. It gives us more of the
man than externals can show—his dreams and
aspirations no less than the scars on his cheek or
the badges on his coat. In a spiritual sense a man
is what he would become if circumstances permitted complete self-realization. The poet's trans-
figured heroes are only men as they idealized
themselves to themselves. We are told that a
friend of Lord Dudley's, reading to him one of
these Conversations, exclaimed upon concluding,
" Is not that exactly what Cicero would have said? "
" Yes, if he could! " was Lord Dudley's answer.

The first division of the Conversations which we
have chosen to make is the Philosophic. After
poet, Landor would perhaps have called himself philosopher. And, though his abilities did
not lie in the direction of abstract thinking,
and though he did not and could not build up
a coherent system of philosophy, his ethical pro-
clivities and his faculty for "the reflective exhibition of certain types of character" led him frequently
to bring the world's great philosophers on the stage.
His professed favorites were Epicurus and Epicte-

tus, though the latter appears in but one brief dialogue. Cicero and Bacon he also admired. His
deep-seated antipathy to Plato is one of the anom-
alies of his character. Few judgments of his
upon the great disciple of Socrates and teacher
of Aristotle,—whom he regards as an unworthy disciple and a dangerous teacher, without wisdom, wit,
or imagination, a mere quibbler "sticking pins in
every chair on which a sophist is likely to sit
down,"—are worthy of serious consideration. But
on the whole we can gather no mean account of the
philosophers and philosophies of antiquity from his
pages.

From the standpoint of art, the philosophic conversations have grave defects. There is too much
consciousness in the manner at times, a suspicion of
fanfaronade—Landor parading his wisdom as, in
one of the dialogues, Lucullus parades his wealth
and Epicurean tastes. There is the lack of con-
secutiveness, too, already noted. It is no excuse to
say that actual conversations rarely have unity of
purpose: an ideal conversation should have,—
therein lies the artist's opportunity. Digression
there may be, but not divagation. When Landor
defended his practice, we may suspect that he was
only attempting to cover a defect.

But this defect becomes still more conspicuous
through another defect, which should have made
unity at least easy to secure. For often there is no
real conversation at all, only a monologue. It is all
give and no take. One character is selected to
become the mouthpiece of certain opinions, while

the secondary character serves merely as a foil or sometimes even as a target. The first speaker declaims, while the second speaker's sole business is to give the cue for each new declamation. Or it may be that the speakers are so much at one in opinion and so destitute of any other characterization that the reader actually finds it immaterial to remember which interlocutor is speaking. Of what use then, we ask, is the dramatic form, except to enable Landor to deliver his opinions without the trouble of organizing them into an essay or treatise? What is gained by attaching the names of Franklin and Washington to general diatribes against national debts or religious dogmas? A conversation should develop and exhibit character, not efface it. Even where dramatic truth is more especially sought by Landor, his characters are likely to be painted with a broad brush and after a very monotonous pattern. The heroic lowly, for example, can seldom conceal their contempt for the powerful, while the powerful are almost without exception blind to heroism and incapable of understanding any motive but selfishness.

Again, a conversation should have animation, diversity,—diversity, that is, of the formal kind, which is yet consistent with unity of substance. Too many of these didactic conversations have not. In other words, Landor the philosopher sometimes drones. We concede it to be the most admirable droning that ever was, but we nod under it none the less. The defect was not wholly temperamental. Landor could be sprightly, after a fashion: no one

who remembers the playful unbending in the
Pentameron or in *Epicurus, Leontion, and Ternissa,*
will deny it. And he could perceive, or feign to
perceive, the defect in Plato: "The voice ought
not to be perpetually nor much elevated in the
ethic and didactic, nor to roll sonorously, as if it
issued from a mask in the theater." But the later
dialogist is scarcely more given to modulation.
Possibly he suspected that his voice was unsteady
on the lower notes. At any rate, he was ready
with a defense: the dialogue of statesmen and
philosophers, he protested, "appertains to disser-
tation and should not resemble the dialogue of
comedians." Nevertheless, we feel that its austerity constitutes the most serious limitation of this
part of his work. We would give a great deal for
more of the comic spirit, the airiness of tone, the
sparkling repartee, that have added so much to the
charm of occasional later experiments in this field
by lesser men.

It is in point of content that this severer portion
of Landor's work yields most to praise. His ethic
bias is everywhere strong. He was a creature of
prejudices; he could not eliminate the personal
equation. And he was overfond of supporting opinions that others reject; he makes Epicurus boast of
having, all his life, planted those roots which other
people dug up and threw away. But when his
heart was right—which was very often, nor is it
hard to detect when—he poured forth that voluminous torrent of noble sentiments which Emerson
summed up, with an unfortunate emphasis upon

their least lovely quality, as "wisdom, wit, and indignation that are unforgetable." In defense of weakness, in scorn of hypocrisy, in praise of justice and magnanimity, he does not weary. He may not give us ultimate truth, truth as distinguished from truths: a philosophy of life, we have said, it was not his to build. Nor does he often descend to the plane of homely wisdom which has been made familiar to us by philosophers like Bacon and Franklin. But in the domain of generous and lofty sentiments, which every man likes to feel that he would cultivate more diligently if only the stress of life allowed, he has given a memorable utterance to perhaps more truths than any other English prose writer. And sometimes too the poet in him triumphs so far over the mere reasoner that he rises to a largeness of truth equaled only by the great poets. "How near together," says Bishop Burnet to Humphrey Hardcastle in a conversation upon the nature of fame, "are things which appear to us the most remote and opposite!—how near to death is life, and vanity to glory! How deceived are we, if our expressions are any proof of it, in what we might deem the very matters most subject to our senses! The haze above our heads we call the heavens, and the thinnest of air the firmament." Passages like these give that strange pause which the mind always suffers under a new revelation.

But largeness of abstract truth and sublimity of utterance are, after all, matters of secondary interest in a world of which man finds or fancies himself the center. However great for us the charm of sentiment in these philosophic dialogues, still greater is the charm of character when character is allowed to appear. For not all of Landor's creatures are marionettes. Now and then the fingers twitch, the eyes light up with sympathy, the voices vibrate with human passion, and we find ourselves on the threshold of the dramatic dialogues with their array of beautiful or commanding personalities so magically summoned to life on this mimic stage. There is the picture of Izaak Walton tarrying on the bridge while his jade winces from the stings of the fly that would make such a delicious morsel for the strawberry-spotted trout or the ash-colored grayling below. There is the same Walton luring himself to a seat on the tulip-pied turf of his friend, the "sunny saint, good master William Oldways." There is Addison as Steele looked back upon him in the days of their friendship, "in his arm-chair, his right hand upon his heart under the fawn-colored waistcoat, his brow erect and clear as his conscience; his wig even and composed as his temper, with measurely curls and antithetical top-knots, like his style; the calmest poet, the most quiet patriot: dear Addison! drunk, deliberate, moral, sentimental, foaming over with truth and virtue, with tenderness and friendship, and only the worse in one ruffle for the wine." There is the figure of Demosthenes as Demosthenes is made to portray it himself, without a single descriptive epithet yet none the less vivid and complete: "I have seen the day, Eubulides, when the most august of cities had but one voice within her walls; and when the stranger on entering them stopped at the silence of the gateway and said, ' Demosthenes is speaking in the assembly of the people.' "

By long contemplation of figures like these, the great and greatly good and greatly wicked of all ages, "shapes of majestic or tumultuous tread," Landor was inevitably led to the construction of those scenes which should portray them at some crucial moment of their lives. These are the Dramatic conversations proper. Helen in the presence of her wronged countryman Achilles, Hannibal in triumph before Marcellus in death, Tiberius torn between filial and husbandly love, Catharine listening outside the door to the murder of her husband, Spenser in desolation, Bacon in disgrace—such are the characters chosen and such are the essentially tragic situations in which they are delineated. The scenes are necessarily brief, and the conversations, scarcely above twenty in all, constitute but a small fraction of the total number, though in every way the most noteworthy fraction. For the poorest are rarely mediocre, engaging an interest that is always near to fascination, while the best of them exhibit Landor's power at its utmost reach.

But before they can be given their right measure of praise, some limits must be noted to their scope and method. One is a limit that inheres in their nature. Drama is not history. This is not the temper in which history is written. There are all the temptations to the imagination, the freedom from responsibility, the desire for effect, that assail the historical romancer. While Landor was little tempted to insincere ostentation, nevertheless the historian is sure to rise and declare, this is not history. No, we can only answer, but it is poetry. And some of us are not without the conviction that fiction may be truer than fact. But, it may be objected, Landor's characters are often not real enough. His Maid of Orleans, his Agnes Sorel, we cannot for a moment imagine to be the real women of history. They are something more than voices, yet scarcely flesh and blood. They are fine in their way, but they are only creatures of imagination—of an imagination that gives them but a mimic, stage life. And it must be admitted that while no man can hope to recreate with entire fidelity an historical character, the dramatist should at least give the illusion of reality. Perhaps here again the fault lies partly in the method. The drama deals more safely with tradition than with history. Wagner, setting about the composition of his great tetralogy, rejected the historical Barbarossa for the legendary Siegfried, and no doubt wisely. Shakespeare's highest conceptions lie outside the pale of history. And the more remotely into history Landor goes, for his Æsop and Rhodopè, his Marcellus and Hannibal, his Leofric and Godiva, the more successful he is.

Yet Landor was not in himself a great dramatist, like Shakespeare, Goethe, Balzac, or even Hugo or Dickens. He wanted the primary requisites, self-effacement and a catholic sympathy. He could not easily get out of himself, and when he could he could not compass the wide range of human life, from Audrey to Cordelia, from Falstaff to Lear. Even within his range he was too prone, as we have seen, to divide men off into classes without allowing for individual distinctions. His priests are nearly all hypocrites who pray for fine weather by the barometer. His women, nobly conceived as some of them are,—Mr. Colvin would set them next to Shakespeare's!—are likely to be now mannish and coarse-fibered, now, in Mr. Colvin's own phrase, "giggly, missish, and disconcerting." These are serious deficiencies. But Landor met them in the only way possible, and met them well. He is content with a character and a passion. He never seeks the motley, nor crowds his stage. In short, it is not drama that he gives us, but a dramatic situation. The situation itself is sometimes tremendous—no weaker word will describe it. Bossuet, before the frivolous Duchess de Fontanges, talks of the frailty of life, and the worn text is transmuted into power by the slipping of a ring from his age-shrunken finger, while its clamorous fall upon the chamber floor reverberates like the thunder of destiny in the ears of the startled girl. It is but an idle criticism of such drama to complain that there is no action. No action is attempted. The characters are not there to do anything, only to be and to suffer. There is neither evolution nor climax, only a crisis—the tension and pause that come when a great soul grapples with fate in an equal conflict. For this, character and passion suffice.

The character, within Landor's limitations, does not fail. Into a character not over subtle or complex, one heroically good or monstrously evil, he entered with ease, for his sympathies, if not broad, were deep. But it is the central fire of passion that suffuses his characters with life, transferring them from the stage of the theater to the stage of the world. Herein lies the secret of his dramatic power, and the quality that differentiates the dramatic dialogues from the philosophic. In the philosophic the characters are mechanically chosen and they always speak from a stage, conscious of their audience. Sometimes they shrink to the thinnest masks, whence only Landor's voice is heard. At best, there is not sufficient passion to humanize and realize them. They move and speak in a rare atmosphere. They seldom condescend, even to each other. Bosom-friends hold intercourse like kings, each hedged by his own divinity, or like the gods fabled by the philosophers, spherical and perfect. We long for some show of emotion, some intimacy, some spontaneous human exchange; but each preserves his inviolate rotundity and the only contact is hard and punctual. There is some compensation in the safety which all this restraint insures. Rebukes, irony, badinage, even a coarse jest, are passed with dignity and a kind of courtesy and good breeding that preclude any fear on the reader's part of a violent ending to the scene. But this is not drama. Nor are the Dramatic dialogues written in any such temper. Occasionally, indeed, even they are marred by something of the same

primness and formality. Unreasoning human impulse is not always allowed to be a sufficient motive
for action—the actor appeals first to the court of
his intellect. "Be seated, O Helena," says Achilles; and Helena complies only with a double
apology: " The feeble are obedient; the weary may
rest even in the presence of the powerful." But
in more inspired moments wisdom itself becomes
warmed, and what would have been a philosophic
abstraction, cold and sententious, from the lips of
Cicero or Epictetus, is glorified by being put into
the mouth of human passion and applied in a crisis
of human life. And when Landor's sympathy is
once wholly engaged, when his characters take
possession of him, and their passions, refined by
suffering, exalted by self-sacrifice, frenzied by
grief, surge beyond his control till he can only
watch and weep over them, as he did over the in-
comparable *Tiberius* and *Vipsania*, the illusion is
complete. Drama and life are one.

The Political and Critical dialogues are upon a
much lower plane. The Political in particular, or
those portions of the more desultory conversations
that touch upon political themes, have little value
of substance and tend too much toward the declama-
tory in style. Mr. Colvin sums the matter up
when he says that in the sphere of politics and
government Landor never got much beyond the
elementary principles of love of freedom and hatred
of tyranny. He had not the civic temperament.
He professed to despise politicians. He was suspicious of the integrity of men in public life. He

never affiliated closely with any party, holding
tenaciously to his own not always consistent views.
He knew the Tories would hate him for his abhor-
rence of the Holy Alliance, the Whigs for his contempt of Napoleon. At Oxford he had worn his
hair without powder ("in a queue tied with black
ribbon") at the risk of being stoned for a republican; and he remained an ardent republican in sentiment all his days. But his instincts were quite too
aristocratic to enable him to go the full length of
democracy. "Let me confess to you," Cleonè
writes to Aspasia, "I do not like your sheer
democracies." The difficulty with him was to rec-
oncile the rights of the individual as represented by
himself with the rights of the individual as represented by the "average man." Monarchy's yoke of
oppression was intolerable, but scarcely less so was
democracy's yoke of equality. He could not, like
Whitman, call every boor brother. With personal
prejudices and poetic sensibilities thus always at
war with an intellectual ideal,—enacting in his own
breast the conflict of Marino Faliero, doge of that
Venice whose republican form of government he
praised as the happiest on earth,—his opinions on
statecraft were not likely to be consistent or con-
vincing. He exalted Prince Louis Napoleon far above
that prince's renowned uncle. His unpleasant experience with English courts of law made him bitter
against English justice. He was fond of satirizing
English institutions in general, though such satire,
put into the mouth of a Russian despot or an absurd
Chinese mandarin, lost much of its effect. He re-

mained provincially British, however, in his hatred of the French, with whom he believed vain-glory, insolence, perfidy, and inhumanity to be ingrained national traits. The French Revolution had been a fine thing to warm the heart of youth, but its agents were wicked, its issues calamitous. France could invent only "her emblematic balloon, the symbol of herself,—flimsy, varnished, inflated, restless, wavering, swaggering." Clearly Landor was no Solon in modern politics. He worked best among the passions that are viewed through the subdued light of centuries. The statesmanship of Pericles, the policy of Athens, the military exploits of Scipio Æmilianus, afforded him more congenial themes.

It would be easy to make light of these defects by regarding them as only the accidents of one kind of greatness, the defects of a quality. Could we for a moment ignore the existence of his strong prejudices, we might really feel that Landor's views upon contemporary politics and history are rendered worthless by the very range of his vision. Not that he was a prophet of the future—in that capacity he succeeded exactly as all others, hitting and missing. Writing in 1824, he made Franklin declare that wars would be impossible among our newly federated States—which nevertheless he lived to see; while in 1851, with an augury to which events in the close of the century are giving at least a passing interest, he anticipated an alliance of America with England, and remarked that the possession of California had opened the Pacific and

Indian seas to the Americans, "who must within the lifetime of some now born predominate in both." But Landor did see the drift of things in the large. "All governments run ultimately into the great gulf of despotism, widen or contract them, straighten or divert them, as you will. From this gulf the Providence that rules all nature liberates them. Again they return, to be again absorbed, at periods not foreseen or calculable." Before this magnificent spectacle of history seen entire, what are all the petty tricks and makeshifts of statecraft, the temporizing and compromising of calculating politicians? At least the eye that could see this may be forgiven for distorting the perspective of nearer objects, and we can understand Landor's assertion that the writing of political dialogues was a most difficult task, since "a man does not lose so much breath by raising his hand above his head as by stooping to tie his shoe-string."

His ventures into the quieter field of literary criticism were in general more successful. It is true he did not understand criticism as we understand it to-day. He came somewhat before Sainte-Beuve and his disciples. Sympathy with an author or his purpose was allowed to play little part. He treated a poem much like a statue, as a detached work of art, a creation of objective beauty in which the moral idea is nothing, the form everything. This means that much of his criticism was spent upon mere technical details, such as words, meters, and sounds. Even a very intelligent and alert reader may be supposed to care little for the slight incongruity of such a phrase as "lips essayed to groan," yet Landor delights in searching a poem of Byron's or Wordsworth's line by line for just such flaws as this. It is like the folly, which he somewhere satirizes, of throwing pin-cushions at the Belvedere Apollo. Nor can we follow him in his rapture over Tibullus because of the latter's "judicious preference of the spondee as one foot of the first hemistich of the pentameter." The criticism may have some value as coming from so expert a classical metrist, but even this is doubtful if the fling at the "skittish Sapphic," which he puts into the mouth of Pollio, be allowable evidence. He spent much time over English spelling and could scarcely be dissuaded from introducing sweeping reforms into his printed works. His prejudices, too, clouded his judgment. He makes Time the final and infallible arbiter of all men's work—except Plato's. He ranked as a great poet his friend Southey, whose gander, Byron declared with characteristic irreverence, he mistook for a swan. He praised Wordsworth until he heard him sneer at Southey's poetry, and then: "Among all the bran in the little bins of Mr. Wordsworth's beer-cellar there is not a legal quart of stout old English beverage." He descends to puerilities. He finds metrical passages in the prose of Demosthenes and rhymes in Plato, though such things can be discovered in any great body of prose, his own not excepted. He carps at the anachronism, in *Paradise Lost*, of Satan's phalanx moving to the Dorian mood, and at Adam's speak-

ing of the sun painting mists with gold when Adam
could know nothing of paint or gold; not seeing
that such strictures, pushed to their logical limit,
would destroy the possibility of putting any words
at all into the mouth of Adam, or of writing any
Paradise Lost. But when all this is said, there
remains much criticism of such a high quality, so
prodigious in range of knowledge and taste, so
judicial and sincere in tone, as to command both
respect and gratitude. He has passed by few of
the world's great writers without some luminous
observation. Many, like Pindar, Catullus, Cicero,
Petrarch, Boccaccio, get quite their full meed of
praise. If he did Scott, Byron, and Wordsworth,
for example, scant justice, he made ample amends
in his generous appreciation of his other contemporaries, Lamb, Keats, Shelley, and Southey, and,
above all, of his earlier countryman through whose
"trumpet burst God's word," his master, Milton.

Touching the style in which this varied matter is
clothed it must be said at once that, could such a
computation be made, Landor's prose would probably be found to unite in itself more excellences with
fewer defects than that of any other English writer.
Other names rise more readily to the lips, because
other men have surpassed him in some specific
quality—Pater in subtle sensuousness, Ruskin in
richness of passionate coloring, De Quincey in
volume of sound, Lamb in sweetness, Milton and
Hooker in sheer pomp of phrase—and we are prone
to judge a man by his highest achievement; but for

artistic balance of many virtues he stands fairly alone. He might even have surpassed some of these in their own qualities had he not held rigorously to an ideal of prose which kept it from invading the province of any other art, and especially poetry. He attained distinction, not by running after strange gods, but by refusing to run after them. He performed the really great feat of achieving individuality of style without mannerism. There is scarcely an ear-mark to know it by, and yet it is all unmistakably Landorian.

Among the pervading qualities which made for this distinction, perhaps the most jealously guarded was originality—an originality that never, of course, degenerated to idiosyncrasy. It is not merely that he avoided the thousand and one phrases which are current in our speech and which serve the journalist so well because they are already perfected and polished and fitted to their place. These are dialect and were necessarily banned for their vulgarity, though possibly there was a degree of snobbishness in such studious banning. But, more than this, his style is almost entirely without a suspicion of indebtedness. Save for a word at rare intervals from the Elizabethans or from the Bible, not a phrase, not a figure, not the turn of a thought, ever suggests a forerunner. If a passage once written was discovered to have a prototype, it was immediately rejected. He carried this independence so far as even to disdain quotation. To disdain it of course was not to escape it. Had he stopped to reflect how relative this matter

is, how far subtler than the mere echoing of words,
he would have realized that there is no escape.
Nevertheless, the instinct to avoid bald quotation
was peculiarly fine and true. Nothing could better
attest his own appreciation of style. Interject
a characteristic phrase from Rossini into one of
Chopin's nocturnes and where is harmony? But
the harmony of tone was purchased dearly. His
proud refusal to draw upon the stores of other
minds leaves his work barren by the side of a
Macaulay's or a Lowell's. He was richer than
these men in his own resources, but he was not
a Shakespeare to stand alone.

The purity of his style is almost as much beyond
question as its originality. He was highly incensed
at those modern authors who permitted themselves
to defile our well of English. He seemed to feel
himself almost alone in his loyalty; Carlyle's
Frederick the Great convinced him that he wrote
"two dead languages—Latin and English." Foreign words he eschewed. New words he was
slow to accept, though he did not, like Macaulay,
affect to scorn a coinage, feeling that "all words
are good which come when they are wanted."
Thus he admitted *Phrygianise;* and he wrote *the-
ophagous* in one edition, though his conservative
fears expunged it in the next. Archaisms found
more favor with him, and the unfamiliar words
which even readers of wide range will come upon
here and there—*pediculous, irrisory, intempestive,
disceptation, pervicacity, roasted*—are mostly of this
class. It is possible, however, that these were

constructed from his knowledge of Latin rather than drawn from his reading in old English. Such is almost certainly the case with the few technical terms of science, like *carious* and *ebulliate*, for he was little interested in the sciences. He had a keen sense of the meaning of words. He was not to be deceived by the poetic glamour of an absurd phrase like "unbidden tears," and he has some-where intimated that "God's anointed" is nothing other than " God's greased."

But there is another quality, not wholly unrelated to originality and purity, which every reader soon learns to associate with Landor's style, and for which perhaps the best name is severity. The presence of the severe eye and the severe hand is manifest on every page. No modern writer has adhered more inflexibly to the Greek ideal of $\mu\eta\delta\grave{\epsilon}\nu$ $\breve{\alpha}\gamma\alpha\nu$—nothing overmuch. Every excrescence of thought, every superfluity of phrase, down to the last particle, is shorn away. The elliptical Pindar and the sententious Bacon excite his approval. Obscurity he professed to abhor, but he abhorred prolixity more, and we are sometimes left face to face with a bare ejaculation and no clew to its meaning. He that runs may not read Landor.

And this compression of matter, which makes him the most aphoristic writer between Bacon and Emerson, is only greater than the vigilant restraint everywhere exercised over form. He was averse from the many rhetorical tricks—hyperbole, bal-ance, repetition, antithesis—that make the stock in trade of more superficially brilliant writers. Whatever was gaudy was to him meretricious and vulgar. Ornament he would have, some remission of severity, but only of the richest—brocade, and never tinsel. In just one direction, perhaps, he relaxed his severity too far. He was tempted to excess of figures, the temptation of the imaginative mind. He held that metaphors should be used sparingly: "that man sees badly who sees everything double." Yet his own metaphors are frequent and full. He resorted most freely to the similitude, which he employed to explain and enforce a foregoing aphorism. Thus, for example, Bacon is made to defend chastity of style:

Something of the severe hath always been appertaining to order and grace ; and the beauty that is not liberal is sought the most ardently and loved the longest. The Graces have their zones, and Venus her cestus.

And thus Agnes Sorel sighs over the instability of love :

Alas ! Alas ! Time loosens man's affections. I may become unworthy. In the sweetest flower there is much that is not fragrance, and which transpires when the freshness has passed away.

Such figures, it must be admitted, have a beauty quite independent of their use. But even of beauty there may be a surfeit. Besides, they are over-refined. They are not wild-flowers of the imagination, but carefully tended plants. They affect us somewhat as Abdul's handmaiden, Almeida, whose human qualities, in Filippo Lippi's description, presented themselves always beneath an exterior "cool, smooth, and firm as a nectarine gathered before sunrise." We feel the allurement, as of something supersensually sensuous, but we are not warmed beyond admiration.

The old question will thrust itself forward here, whether we are to range Landor with the classic or with the romantic writers. Critics cannot quite agree, though usually uniting with Mr. Colvin in placing him on the classic side. Surely the matter, though not simple, is clear. There were two men in Landor—one of very romantic temper, which was always rising to the surface and impressing itself upon those who came into casual contact with him; the other, serene and self-controlled, reserved for his few intimate friends, and betrayed to the world only in his works of purest art. Right here indeed is the main wonder, that a man of such tremendous energies, such perverse and impetuous self-will, should achieve this well-nigh absolute restraint. Passionate, rebellious, individualistic by nature, when he approaches his art how calm and conservative! how he ranges his forces on the side of law and order, confronting the barbarian hordes of the romanticists with a solid Macedonian phalanx! For classicism means predominance of intellect and the sense for artistic restraint, while romanticism means predominance of emotion and the impulse toward natural freedom. The one makes for definiteness of conception, severity of form, simplicity, purity, permanence; the other for subtlety of impression, riot of color, exuberance, lawlessness, change. It is not that Landor totally repressed his romantic tendencies. They show quite frequently enough to account for the confusion of critics. It would be strange indeed if no traces of the man who echoed the republican sentiments of Milton and lauded the sensuous art of Keats should be found in all his voluminous works, professedly dramatic and objective though they be. And the traces are there—now in a touch of most delicate nature-feeling, now in a bit of arabesque description, now in a cry of very human passion. But for the most part Landor the artist sits above unmoved, judging and regulating.

This will go far, too, toward explaining his unique position—apart from men of the second order of genius, yet distinctly below those of the first. He aimed to stand with the latter in possessing both the romantic and the classic temper and preserving them in perfect balance. Or, as he might have formulated to himself what was of course never a distinctly conscious aim, he tried to maintain a richly endowed nature in harmonious development. Thus far he succeeded, but unfortunately his intellect was not of the first order. Had he realized this and given free play to his romantic tendencies, he would have attracted at once that wide public which is always susceptible to emotional appeals and is caught by glitter and noise. But he set his face the other way, subduing his nature to the measure of his intellect and aspiring to the company of Homer and Shakespeare. The balance was secured, but the companionship must be denied, for he lacked the highest attribute of pure intellect, the faculty for synthesis and organization, without which no depth or fervor of imagination can produce a transcendent work of art.

So far as mere style goes, the effect of this classic restraint is disappointing upon all but those who rejoice in the gift, or suffer under the affliction, of what pathology knows as hyperæsthesia. The recently discovered Delphic hymn to Apollo seems to us strangely monotonous in its melody. But it is only a type of all Greek art. The modulation is there, so surely as the entasis is in the shaft of the Doric column, though our ears and eyes, long dulled by the violences done in the name of romanticism, may need a requickening to perceive them. So there are modulations in Landor's art—condescensions enough to ear and eye. There are no bursts of sound, it may be, but there is mellifluous music everywhere and scarcely a sentence that is not tuneful. And the monotint of many a somber passage is relieved by an exquisite picture, clear in outline as a vase-painting and delicately colored as an aquarelle. Quite beyond any graphic art indeed is Petrarca's limning of "the peculiar and costly decoration of our Tuscan villas: the central turret, round which the kite perpetually circles in search of pigeons or smaller prey, borne onward, like the Flemish skater, by effortless will in motionless progression." Or take this from the only tedious story that Chaucer ever told:

Soon however that quarter of the field began to show its herbage again in larger spaces ; and at the distant sound of the French trumpets, which was shrill, fitful, and tuneless, the broken ranks of the enemy near him waved like a tattered banner in the wind, and melted, and disappeared.

One thing, however, which Landor intended as an amenity of his style must be rated as a serious defect. It is a pity that he did not estimate more rightly his poor gift for humor. Purely as humor, it is not often acceptable. As just intimated, he puts a tale into the mouth of Chaucer which might almost perturb the rest of that gentle spirit. And the humor is made inexpressibly worse when it descends to indelicacy—one of the manifestations of what Arnold has called, with less than his usual felicity, "the provincial note." We remember, of course, that he was a child of the eighteenth century, of an age considerably less sensitive than ours. And he grew more scrupulous as he grew older, canceling here and there. But enough remains to give every sensitive reader pain. When, for example, Achilles tells how his father went with the brothers of Helena to hunt the boar in the brakes of Kalydon, and Helena responds, "Horrible creatures!—boars I mean," we can but sympathize with Mr. Colvin's desire to suppress the irrelevant exclamation. Again, toward the end of the conversation between Fra Filippo Lippi and Pope Eugenius the Fourth there is a passage that may well be quoted here, so typical is it throughout of Landor's genius, in which the proudest strength but too often betrays some fatal weakness.

Filippo. In the beautiful little town of Prato, reposing in its illness against the hill that protects it from the north, and looking over fertile meadows, southward to Poggio Cajano, westward to Pistoja, there is the convent of Santa Margarita. I was invited by the sisters to paint an altar-piece for the chapel. A novice of fifteen, my own sweet Lucrezia, came one day alone to see me work at my Madonna. Her blessed countenance had already looked down on every beholder lower by the knees. I myself, who had made her, could almost have worshiped her.

Eugenius. Not while incomplete ; no half-virgin will do.

Filippo. But there knelt Lucrezia ! there she knelt ! first looking with devotion at the Madonna, then with admiring wonder and grateful delight at the artist. Could so little a heart be divided ? Twere a pity ! There was enough for me : there is never enough for the Madonna. Resolving on a sudden that the object of my love should be the object of adoration to thousands, born and unborn, I swept my brush across the maternal face, and left a blank in heaven. The little girl screamed : I pressed her to my bosom.

No praise would seem extravagant for this narrative of Filippo's, which comes upon a jaded literary taste with a pleasure so exquisite, so intense, as scarcely to be described but in terms of pain. And then to have it marred by that inane jest! Was there no other way in which Landor could satisfy his desire to ridicule the pope? It is the brush across the Madonna's face. The feeling it arouses is deeper than irritation, it is poignant sorrow. *The pity of it !* we say, as when we gaze on the mutilated Venus of Milo. Only there it is the void, the defect, here it is the blemish. Where so much else is perfect to the last touch, why not all? The artist's taste was never sure, even when his art was at its highest.

But the nice adjustment of these conflicting claims becomes an endless and idle task. The

balance has already been struck, and we must con-
clude as we began. Speaking of his fame, Landor
declared, in words which no critic can refrain from
quoting: "I shall dine late; but the dining-room
will be well lighted, the guests few and select." By
attempting thus to anticipate the verdict of pos-
terity, he only hampered and delayed that verdict.
For it has been hard to treat dispassionately one
who could rarely be dispassionate, hard not to be
either roused to antagonism or moved to disdain.
But a few years suffice to remove such obstructions,
and we see clearly enough now that Landor was
right. Fame is at best a foolish thing, the world's
unhonored note for value received, but we know
what measure of it falls to this man. Without
Carlyle's strenuous insistence upon conduct, without Arnold's anxious concern for truth, without
Ruskin's passionate worship of beauty, it was yet
his to combine in some degree the virtues of all and
to present both precepts of wisdom and inspiration
to noble life under forms of imperishable beauty
and power.

CHRONOLOGY.

1775. Landor born at Warwick, January 30.

c. 1779. To school at Knowle.

c. 1785. To Rugby.

1793. A commoner at Trinity College, Oxford.

1794-98. London and Wales.

1799-1808. Chiefly at Bath.

1808. With the army in Spain.

1811. Marries Julia Thuillier. At Llanthony Abbey, Monmouthshire.

1814. To Tours.

1815-35. In Italy : Como, Pisa, Pistoia, Florence (1821), Fiesole (Villa Gherardesca, 1829).

1835-58. In England, chiefly at Bath.

1858-64. In Italy : Fiesole, Siena, Florence (1859).

1864. Died at Florence, September 17.

BIBLIOGRAPHY.

1795. Poems.
1798. Gebir ; a Poem in Seven Books.
1800. Poems from the Arabic and Persian.
1803. Gebirus. [The Latin version of Gebir].
1806. Simonidea.
1812. Count Julian : a Tragedy.
1815. Idyllia nova quinque Heroum atque Heroidum. Oxford.
1820. Idyllia Heroica decem. Pisa.
1824-29. Imaginary Conversations of Literary Men and Statesmen, etc. London. Vols. i. and ii., 1824; second ed., corrected and enlarged, 1826. Vol. iii., 1828. Vols. iv. and v., 1829.
1834. Citation and Examination of William Shakespeare.
1836. Pericles and Aspasia.
1837. The Pentameron and Pentalogia.
1839. Andrea of Hungary and Giovanna of Naples.
1841. Fra Rupert.
1847. Poemata et Inscriptiones.
1847. The Hellenics. (Translations of the Idyllia with additions.)
1853. The Last Fruit off an Old Tree.
1858. Dry Sticks, fagoted by Walter Savage Landor.
1859. The Hellenics. Enlarged.
1863. Heroic Idyls, with additional poems.

1846. Works. London, 2 vols.
1876. Works and Life. Ed. by John Forster. London. 8 vols. The prose works were reprinted 1883 ss, Boston, 7 vols.

1891–92. Works. Ed. by C. G. Crump. London, 10 vols. Variorum edition, with notes; text based on Forster.

1882. Selections. Arr. and ed. by Sidney Colvin. London.

Selections have also been edited by G. ·S. Hillard, Boston, 1856; by Havelock Ellis, London, 1886 (Pentameron, 1889, Pericles and Aspasia, 1890); by W. B. S. Clymer, Boston, 1898.

BIOGRAPHY AND CRITICISM.

Walter Savage Landor; a Biography. By John Forster. London, 2 vols., 1869. Revised and printed as vol. i. of 1876 ed. of Works and Life. New ed., 1895. Authorized, full, frank, trustworthy, but cumbrous and often uncritical.

Landor. By Sidney Colvin. English Men of Letters. London, 1884. Condensed, precise, discriminating.

Some Letters to Miss Mary Boyle. Century, Feb., 1888.

Letters and other Unpublished Writings of Walter Savage Landor. Ed. by Stephen Wheeler. London, 1897. Contains a full bibliography.

Letters of Walter Savage Landor, Private and Public. Ed. by Stephen Wheeler. London, 1899.

See also *Landor* in Ency. Brit. by Mr. Swinburne, and in Dict. of Nat. Biog. by Mr. Leslie Stephen. Also Leigh Hunt's *Lord Byron and his Contemporaries,* 1827; Countess of Blessington's *Idler in Italy,* 1839; Horne's *New Spirit of the Age* (art. partly by Miss Barrett), 1844; Madden's *Lit. Life and Corr. of Countess of Blessington,* 1855; Emerson's *English Traits,* 1856; Kate Field's *Last Days of Landor, Atl. Mo.,* 1866; Crabb Robinson's *Diary,* 1869; Chas. Dickens in *All the Year Round,* 1869; Mrs. E. Lynn Linton's *Reminiscences* in *Fraser's,* 1870; Lord Houghton's *Monographs,* 1873; *The Landor-Blessington Papers* in Nicoll and Wise's *Literary Anecdotes of the Nineteenth Century,* London, 1896; and *An Open Letter to R. W. Emerson,* in the same.

de Vere, Aubrey. *Landor's Poetry.* Essays, Chiefly on Poetry, 1887.

Dowden, Edward. *Studies in Literature.* London, 1892. A study of Landor's temperament and art.

Lowell, J. R. *Latest Literary Essays.* Article written as introduction to the Letters of Landor in the *Century*, 1888.

Scudder, Horace E. *Landor as a Classic.* Men and Letters. Boston, 1887.

Stedman, E. C. *Victorian Poets.* Boston, 1875.

Stephen, Leslie. *Hours in a Library*, 1879. A temperate review of the style and motive of the Imaginary Conversations.

Swinburne, A. C. *Song for the Centenary of Walter Savage Landor.* A dithyrambic summary and eulogy of Landor's life and work.

Woodberry, G. E. *Atl. Monthly*, vol. 51. *Studies in Letters and Life*, Boston, 1890. The " objective " character of Landor's work is given emphasis.

See also the critical introductions to the various editions of works and selections.

IMAGINARY CONVERSATIONS.

Aesop and Rhodope.

Æsop. And so, our fellow-slaves are given to contention on the score of dignity?

Rhodope. I do not believe they are much addicted to contention; for, whenever the good Xanthus
5 hears a signal of such misbehaviour, he either brings a scourge into the midst of them, or sends our lady to scold them smartly for it.

Æsop. Admirable evidence against their propensity!

10 *Rhodope*. I will not have you find them out so, nor laugh at them.

Æsop. Seeing that the good Xanthus and our lady are equally fond of thee, and always visit thee both together, the girls, however envious, cannot
15 well or safely be arrogant, but must of necessity yield the first place to thee.

Rhodope. They indeed are observant of the kindness thus bestowed upon me; yet they afflict me by taunting me continually with what I am un-
20 able to deny.

Æsop. If it is true, it ought little to trouble thee; if untrue, less. I know, for I have looked

into nothing else of late, no evil can thy heart have
admitted: a sigh of thine before the gods would
remove the heaviest that could fall on it.   Pray
tell me what it may be.   Come, be courageous; be
cheerful!   I can easily pardon a smile if thou em- 5
pleadest me of curiosity.

Rhodopè. They remark to me that enemies or
robbers took them forcibly from their parents—
and that—and that——

Æsop. Likely enough: what then? Why desist 10
from speaking? why cover thy face with thy hair
and hands? Rhodopè! Rhodopè! dost thou weep,
moreover?

Rhodopè. It is so sure!

Æsop. Was the fault thine?   15

Rhodopè. O that it were!—if there was any.

Æsop. While it pains thee to tell it, keep thy
silence; but when utterance is a solace, then im-
part it.

Rhodopè. They remind me (oh! who could have 20
had the cruelty to relate it) that my father, my own
dear father——

Æsop. Say not the rest: I know it: his day has
come.

Rhodopè. —sold me, sold me. You start; you did 25
not at the lightning last night, nor at the rolling
sounds above. And do you, generous Æsop! do
you also call a misfortune a disgrace?

Æsop. If it is, I am among the most disgraceful
of men. Didst thou dearly love thy father?   30

Rhodopè. All loved him. He was very fond of
me.

Æsop. And yet sold thee! sold thee to a stranger!
Rhodopè. He was the kindest of all kind fathers,
nevertheless. Nine summers ago, you may have
heard perhaps, there was a grievous famine in our
5 land of Thrace.

Æsop. I remember it perfectly.

Rhodopè. O poor Æsop! and were you too fam-
ishing in your native Phrygia?

Æsop. The calamity extended beyond the narrow
10 sea that separates our countries. My appetite was
sharpened; but the appetite and the wits are
equally set on the same grindstone.

Rhodopè. I was then scarcely five years old; my
mother died the year before: my father sighed at
15 every funeral, but he sighed more deeply at every
bridal, song. He loved me because he loved her
who bore me: and yet I made him sorrowful whether
I cried or smiled. If ever I vexed him, it was because I would not play when he told me, but
20 made him, by my weeping, weep again.

Æsop. And yet he could endure to lose thee! he,
thy father! Could any other? could any who lives
on the fruits of the earth, endure it? O age, that
art incumbent over me! blessed be thou; thrice
25 blessed! Not that thou stillest the tumults of the
heart, and promisest eternal calm, but that, pre-
vented by thy beneficence, I never shall experience
this only intolerable wretchedness.

Rhodopè. Alas! alas!

30 *Æsop.* Thou art now happy, and shouldst not
utter that useless exclamation.

Rhodopè. You said something angrily and vehe-

mently when you stepped aside. Is it not enough
that the handmaidens doubt the kindness of my
father? Must so virtuous and so wise a man as
Æsop blame him also?

Æsop. Perhaps he is little to be blamed; certainly 5
he is much to be pitied.

Rhodopè. Kind heart! on which mine must never
rest!

Æsop. Rest on it for comfort and for counsel
when they fail thee: rest on it, as the deities on 10
the breast of mortals, to console and purify it.

Rhodopè. Could I remove any sorrow from it, I
should be contented.

Æsop. Then be so; and proceed in thy narrative. 15

Rhodopè. Bear with me a little yet. My thoughts
have overpowered my words, and now themselves
are overpowered and scattered. Forty-seven days
ago (this is only the forty-eighth since I beheld you
first) I was a child; I was ignorant, I was care- 20
less.

Æsop. If these qualities are signs of childhood,
the universe is a nursery.

Rhodopè. Affliction, which makes many wiser,
had no such effect on me. But reverence and love 25
(why should I hesitate at the one avowal more than
at the other?) came over me, to ripen my understanding.

Æsop. O Rhodopè! we must loiter no longer
upon this discourse. 30

Rhodopè. Why not?

Æsop. Pleasant is yonder beanfield, seen over

the high papyrus when it waves and bends: deep
laden with the sweet heaviness of its odour is the
listless air that palpitates dizzily above it; but
Death is lurking for the slumberer beneath its
5 blossoms.

Rhodopè. You must not love then!—but may
not I?

Æsop. We will,—but——

Rhodopè. We! O sound that is to vibrate on my
10 breast for ever! O hour, happier than all other
hours since time began! O gracious gods! who
brought me into bondage!

Æsop. Be calm, be composed, be circumspect.
We must hide our treasure that we may not lose it.

15 *Rhodopè.* I do not think that you can love me; and
I fear and tremble to hope so. Ah, yes; you have
said you did. But again you only look at me, and
sigh as if you repented.

Æsop. Unworthy as I may be of thy fond regard,
20 I am not unworthy of thy fullest confidence: why
distrust me?

Rhodopè. Never will I!—never, never! To know
that I possess your love surpasses all other knowledge, dear as is all that I receive from you. I
25 should be tired of my own voice if I heard it on
aught beside: and even yours is less melodious
in any other sound than *Rhodopè.*

Æsop. Do such little girls learn to flatter?

Rhodopè. Teach me how to speak, since you
30 could not teach me how to be silent.

Æsop. Speak no longer of me, but of thyself;
and only of things that never pain thee.

Rhodopè. Nothing can pain me now.

Æsop. Relate thy story then, from infancy.

Rhodopè. I must hold your hand: I am afraid of losing you again.

Æsop. Now begin. Why silent so long?   5

Rhodopè. I have dropped all memory of what is told by me and what is untold.

Æsop. Recollect a little. I can be patient with this hand in mine.

Rhodopè. I am not certain that yours is any help 10 to recollection.

Æsop. Shall I remove it?

Rhodopè. O! now I think I can recall the whole story. What did you say? did you ask any question?   15

Æsop. None, excepting what thou hast answered.

Rhodopè. Never shall I forget the morning when my father, sitting in the coolest part of the house, exchanged his last measure of grain for a chlamys of scarlet cloth fringed with silver. He watched 20 the merchant out of the door, and then looked wistfully into the corn-chest. I, who thought there was something worth seeing, looked in also, and, finding it empty, expressed my disappointment, not thinking, however, about the corn. A 25 faint and transient smile came over his countenance at the sight of mine. He unfolded the chlamys, stretched it out with both hands before me, and then cast it over my shoulders. I looked down on the glittering fringe and screamed with joy. He 30 then went out; and I know not what flowers he gathered, but he gathered many; and some he

placed in my bosom, and some in my hair. But I
told him with captious pride, first that I could
arrange them better, and again that I would have
only the white. However, when he had selected all
5 the white, and I had placed a few of them according to my fancy, I told him (rising in my slipper)
he might crown me with the remainder. The splen-
dour of my apparel gave me a sensation of authority. Soon as the flowers had taken their station
10 on my head, I expressed a dignified satisfaction at
the taste displayed by my father, just as if I could
have seen how they appeared! But he knew that
there was at least as much pleasure as pride in it,
and perhaps we divided the latter (alas! not both)
15 pretty equally. He now took me into the market-
place, where a concourse of people was waiting
for the purchase of slaves. Merchants came and
looked at me; some commending, others disparag-
ing; but all agreeing that I was slender and
20 delicate, that I could not live long, and that I
should give much trouble. Many would have
bought the chlamys, but there was something less
salable in the child and flowers.

Æsop. Had thy features been coarse and thy
25 voice rustic, they would all have patted thy cheeks
and found no fault in thee.

Rhodopè. As it was, every one had bought exactly such another in time past, and been a loser by
it. At these speeches I perceived the flowers trem-
30 ble slightly on my bosom, from my father's agitation.
Although he scoffed at them, knowing my healthi-
ness, he was troubled internally, and said many

short prayers, not very unlike imprecations, turning
his head aside. Proud was I, prouder than ever,
when at last several talents were offered for me,
and by the very man who in the beginning had un-
dervalued me the most, and prophesied the worst 5
of me. My father scowled at him, and refused the
money. I thought he was playing a game, and
began to wonder what it could be, since I never had
seen it played before. Then I fancied it might be
some celebration because plenty had returned to 10
the city, insomuch that my father had bartered the
last of the corn he hoarded. I grew more and more
delighted at the sport. But soon there advanced
an elderly man, who said gravely, "Thou hast
stolen this child: her vesture alone is worth above 15
a hundred drachmas. Carry her home again to her
parents, and do it directly, or Nemesis and the
Eumenides will overtake thee." Knowing the estimation in which my father had always been holden
by his fellow-citizens, I laughed again, and pinched 20
his ear. He, although naturally choleric, burst
forth into no resentment at these reproaches, but
said calmly, "I think I know thee by name, O
guest! Surely thou art Xanthus the Samian. Deliver this child from famine."   25

Again I laughed aloud and heartily; and thinking
it was now my part of the game, I held out both my
arms and protruded my whole body toward the
stranger. He would not receive me from my
father's neck, but he asked me with benignity and 30
solicitude if I was hungry; at which I laughed
again, and more than ever; for it was early in the

morning, soon after the first meal, and my father had nourished me most carefully and plentifully in all the days of the famine. But Xanthus, waiting for no answer, took out of a sack, which one of his 5 slaves carried at his side, a cake of wheaten bread and a piece of honey-comb, and gave them to me. I held the honey-comb to my father's mouth, thinking it the most of a dainty. He dashed it to the ground; but, seizing the bread, he began to devour 10 it ferociously. This also I thought was in play; and I clapped my hands at his distortions. But Xanthus looked on him like one afraid, and smote the cake from him, crying aloud, "Name the price." My father now placed me in his arms, naming a 15 price much below what the other had offered, saying, "The gods are ever with thee, O Xanthus! therefore to thee do I consign my child." But while Xanthus was counting out the silver, my father seized the cake again, which the slave had 20 taken up and was about to replace in the wallet. His hunger was exasperated by the taste and the delay. Suddenly there arose much tumult. Turning round in the old woman's bosom who had received me from Xanthus, I saw my beloved father strug-25 gling on the ground, livid and speechless. The more violent my cries, the more rapidly they hurried me away; and many were soon between us. Little was I suspicious that he had suffered the pangs of famine long before: alas! and he had suffered them 30 for me. Do I weep while I am telling you they ended? I could not have closed his eyes; I was too young: but I might have received his last breath,

the only comfort of an orphan's bosom. Do you
now think him blamable, O . Esop?

Esop. It was sublime humanity: it was forbearance and self-denial which even the immortal gods
have never shown us. He could endure to perish 5
by those torments which alone are both acute and
slow; he could number the steps of death and miss
not one: but he could never see thy tears, nor let
thee see his. O weakness above all fortitude!
Glory to the man who rather bears a grief corroding 10
his breast, than permits it to prowl beyond, and to
prey on the tender and compassionate! Women
commiserate the brave, and men the beautiful. The
dominion of Pity has usually this extent, no wider.
Thy father was exposed to the obloquy not only of 15
the malicious, but also of the ignorant and thoughtless, who condemn in the unfortunate what they ap-
plaud in the prosperous. There is no shame in
poverty or in slavery, if we neither make ourselves
poor by our improvidence nor slaves by our venality. 20
The lowest and highest of the human race are
sold: most of the intermediate are also slaves, but
slaves who bring no money in the market.

Rhodopè. Surely the great and powerful are never
to be purchased, are they?   25

Esop. It may be a defect in my vision, but I
cannot see greatness on the earth. What they tell
me is great and aspiring, to me seems little and
crawling. Let me meet thy question with another.
What monarch gives his daughter for nothing? 30
Either he receives stone walls and unwilling cities in
return, or he barters her for a parcel of spears and

horses and horsemen, waving away from his declining and helpless age young joyous life, and tramp-
ling down the freshest and the sweetest memories.
Midas in the height of prosperity would have given
5 his daughter to Lycaon, rather than to the gentlest,
the most virtuous, the most intelligent of his subjects. Thy father threw wealth aside, and placing
thee under the protection of Virtue, rose up from
the house of Famine to partake in the festivals of
10 the gods.

Release my neck, O Rhodopè! for I have other
questions to ask of thee about him.

Rhodopè. To hear thee converse on him in such
a manner I can do even that.   •

15 *Æsop.* Before the day of separation was he never
sorrowful? Did he never by tears or silence reveal
the secret of his soul?

Rhodopè. I was too infantine to perceive or imagine his intention. The night before I became the
20 slave of Xanthus, he sat on the edge of my bed. I
pretended to be asleep: he moved away silently and
softly. I saw him collect in the hollow of his hand
the crumbs I had wasted on the floor, and then eat
them, and then look if any were remaining. I
25 thought he did so out of fondness for me, remem-
bering that, even before the famine, he had often
swept up off the table the bread I had broken, and
had made me put it between his lips. I would not
dissemble very long, but said,—

30 "Come, now you have wakened me, you must
sing me asleep again, as you did when I was little."

He smiled faintly at this, and, after some delay,

when he had walked up and down the chamber, thus
began:—

"I will sing to thee one song more, my wakeful
Rhodopè! my chirping bird! over whom is no
mother's wing! That it may lull thee asleep, I 5
will celebrate no longer, as in the days of wine and
plenteousness, the glory of Mars, guiding in their
invisibly rapid onset the dappled steeds of Rhæsus.
What hast thou to do, my little one, with arrows
tired of clustering in the quiver? How much 10
quieter is thy pallet than the tents which whitened
the plain of Simöis! What knowest thou about
the river Eurotas? What knowest thou about its
ancient palace, once trodden by assembled gods,
and then polluted by the Phrygian? What knowest 15
thou of perfidious men or of sanguinary deeds?

"Pardon me, O goddess who presidest in Cy-
thera! I am not irreverent to thee, but ever grateful. May she upon whose brow I lay my hand
praise and bless thee for evermore!   20

"Ah, yes! continue to hold up above the cover-
let those fresh and rosy palms clasped together: her
benefits have descended on thy beauteous head, my
child! The Fates also have sung, beyond thy hearing, of pleasanter scenes than snow-fed Hebrus; of 25
more than dim grottoes and sky-bright waters.
Even now a low murmur swells upward to my ear:
and not from the spindle comes the sound, but
from those who sing slowly over it, bending all
three their tremulous heads together. I wish thou 30
couldst hear it; for seldom are their voices so sweet.
Thy pillow intercepts the song perhaps: lie down

again, lie down, my Rhodopè! I will repeat what
they are saying:—

" ' Happier shalt thou be, nor less glorious, than
even she, the truly beloved, for whose return to the
5 distaff and the lyre the portals of Tænarus flew open.
In the woody dells of Ismarus, and when she bathed
among the swans of Strymon, the nymphs called
her Eurydicè. Thou shalt behold that fairest and
that fondest one hereafter. But first thou must
10 go into the land of the lotos, where famine never
cometh, and where alone the works of man are
immortal.'

"O my child! the undeceiving Fates have uttered
this. Other powers have visited me, and have
15 strengthened my heart with dreams and visions.
We shall meet again, my Rhodopè! in shady groves
and verdant meadows, and we shall sit by the side
of those who loved us."

He was rising: I threw my arms about his neck,
20 and, before I would let him go, I made him promise
to place me, not by the side, but between them; for
I thought of her who had left us. At that time
there were but two, O Æsop!

You ponder: you are about to reprove my assur-
25 ance in having thus repeated my own praises. I
would have omitted some of the words, only that it
might have disturbed the measure and cadences,
and have put me out. They are the very words my
dearest father sang; and they are the last. Yet,
30 shame upon me! the nurse (the same who stood listening near, who attended me into this country)
could remember them more perfectly: it is from

her I have learned them since; she often sings
them, even by herself.

Æsop. So shall others.   There is much both in
them and in thee to render them memorable.

Rhodopè. Who flatters now?   5

Æsop. Flattery often runs beyond Truth, in a
hurry to embrace her; but not here.   The dullest
of mortals, seeing and hearing thee, could never
misinterpret the prophecy of the Fates.

If, turning back, I could overpass the vale of 10
years, and could stand on the mountain-top, and
could look again far before me at the bright ascending morn, we would enjoy the prospect together;
we would walk along the summit hand in hand, O
Rhodopè! and we would only sigh at last when we 15
found ourselves below with others.

Marcellus and Hannibal.

Hannibal. Could a Numidian horseman ride no faster? Marcellus! ho! Marcellus! He moves not —he is dead. Did he not stir his fingers? Stand wide, soldiers—wide, forty paces—give him air— 5 bring water—halt! Gather those broad leaves, and all the rest, growing under the brushwood—unbrace his armour. Loose the helmet first—his breast rises. I fancied his eyes were fixed on me—they have rolled back again. Who presumed to touch my shoulder? 10 This horse? It was surely the horse of Marcellus! Let no man mount him. Ha! ha! the Romans, too, sink into luxury: here is gold about the charger.

Gaulish Chieftain. Execrable thief! The golden chain of our king under a beast's grinders! The ven- 15 geance of the gods hath overtaken the impure——

Hannibal. We will talk about vengeance when we have entered Rome, and about purity among the priests, if they will hear us. Sound for the surgeon. That arrow may be extracted from the side, deep 20 as it is.—The conqueror of Syracuse lies before me. —Send a vessel off to Carthage. Say Hannibal is at the gates of Rome.—Marcellus, who stood alone between us, fallen. Brave man! I would rejoice and cannot.—How awfully serene a countenance! 25 Such as we hear are in the Islands of the Blessed. And how glorious a form and stature! Such too

was theirs!   They also once lay thus upon the earth
wet with their blood—few other enter there.   And
what plain armour!

Gaulish Chieftain. My party slew him—indeed I
think I slew him myself.   I claim the chain: it be- 5
longs to my king; the glory of Gaul requires it.
Never will she endure to see another take it: rather
would she lose her last man.   We swear! we swear!

Hannibal. My friend, the glory of Marcellus did
not require him to wear it.   When he suspended the 10
arms of your brave king in the temple, he thought
such a trinket unworthy of himself and of Jupiter.
The shield he battered down, the breast-plate he
pierced with his sword—these he showed to the
people and to the gods; hardly his wife and little 15
children saw this, ere his horse wore it.

Gaulish Chieftain. Hear me, O Hannibal!

Hannibal. What! when Marcellus lies before me?
when his life may perhaps be recalled? when I may
lead him in triumph to Carthage? when Italy, Sicily, 20
Greece, Asia, wait to obey me? Content thee! I
will give thee mine own bridle, worth ten such.

Gaulish Chieftain. For myself?

Hannibal. For thyself.

Gaulish Chieftain.   And these rubies and emeralds, 25
and that scarlet——

Hannibal. Yes, yes.

Gaulish Chieftain. O glorious Hannibal! unconquerable hero! O my happy country! to have such
an ally and defender.   I swear eternal gratitude— 30
yes, gratitude, love, devotion, beyond eternity.

Hannibal. In all treaties we fix the time: I could

hardly ask a longer. Go back to thy station.—I would see what the surgeon is about, and hear what he thinks. The life of Marcellus! the triumph of Hannibal! what else has the world in it? Only
5 Rome and Carthage: these follow.

Surgeon. Hardly an hour of life is left.

Marcellus. I must die then! The gods be praised! The commander of a Roman army is no captive.

Hannibal (to the Surgeon). Could not he bear a
10 sea-voyage? Extract the arrow.

Surgeon. He expires that moment.

Marcellus. It pains me: extract it.

Hannibal. Marcellus, I see no expression of pain on your countenance, and never will I consent to hasten
15 the death of an enemy in my power. Since your recovery is hopeless, you say truly you are no captive.

(*To the Surgeon.*) Is there nothing, man, that can assuage the mortal pain? for, suppress the signs of it as he may, he must feel it. Is there nothing to
20 alleviate and allay it?

Marcellus. Hannibal, give me thy hand—thou hast found it and brought it me, compassion.

(*To the Surgeon.*) Go, friend; others want thy aid; several fell around me.

25 *Hannibal.* Recommend to your country, O Marcellus, while time permits it, reconciliation and peace with me, informing the Senate of my superiority in force, and the impossibility of resistance. The tablet is ready: let me take off this ring—try
30 to write, to sign it at least. Oh, what satisfaction I feel at seeing you able to rest upon the elbow, and even to smile!

Marcellus. Within an hour or less, with how severe a brow would Minos say to me, " Marcellus, is this thy writing?"

Rome loses one man: she hath lost many such, and she still hath many left.   5

Hannibal. Afraid as you are of falsehood, say you this? I confess in shame the ferocity of my countrymen. Unfortunately, too, the nearer posts are occupied by Gauls, infinitely more cruel. The Numidians are so in revenge; the Gauls both in 10 revenge and in sport. My presence is required at a distance, and I apprehend the barbarity of one or other, learning, as they must do, your refusal to execute my wishes for the common good, and feeling that by this refusal you deprive them of their 15 country, after so long an absence.

Marcellus. Hannibal, thou art not dying.

Hannibal. What then? What mean you?

Marcellus. That thou mayest, and very justly, have many things yet to apprehend: I can have 20 none. The barbarity of thy soldiers is nothing to me: mine would not dare be cruel. Hannibal is forced to be absent; and his authority goes away with his horse. On this turf lies defaced the semblance of a general; but Marcellus is yet the 25 regulator of his army. Dost thou abdicate a power conferred on thee by thy nation? Or wouldst thou acknowledge it to have become, by thy own sole fault, less plenary than thy adversary's?

I have spoken too much: let me rest; this mantle 30 oppresses me.

Hannibal. I placed my mantle on your head when

the helmet was first removed, and while you were
lying in the sun. Let me fold it under, and then
replace the ring.

Marcellus. Take it, Hannibal. It was given me
5 by a poor woman who flew to me at Syracuse, and
who covered it with her hair, torn off in desperation
that she had no other gift to offer. Little thought
I that her gift and her words should be mine. How
suddenly may the most powerful be in the situation
10 of the most helpless! Let that ring and the mantle
under my head be the exchange of guests at parting.
The time may come, Hannibal, when thou (and the
gods alone know whether as conqueror or conquered) mayest sit under the roof of my children,
15 and in either case it shall serve thee. In thy
adverse fortune, they will remember on whose
pillow their father breathed his last; in thy prosperous (Heaven grant it may shine upon thee in
some other country!) it will rejoice thee to protect
20 them. We feel ourselves the most exempt from
affliction when we relieve it, although we are then
the most conscious that it may befall us.

There is one thing here which is not at the dis-
posal of either.

25 *Hannibal.* What?

Marcellus. This body.

Hannibal. Whither would you be lifted? Men
are ready.

Marcellus. I meant not so. My strength is fail-
30 ing. I seem to hear rather what is within than
what is without. My sight and my other senses
are in confusion. I would have said—This body,

when a few bubbles of air shall have left it, is no more worthy of thy notice than of mine; but thy glory will not let thee refuse it to the piety of my family.

Hannibal. You would ask something else.   I per-   5 ceive an inquietude not visible till now.

Marcellus. Duty and Death make us think of home sometimes.

Hannibal. Thitherward the thoughts of the con-queror and of the conquered fly together.   10

Marcellus. Hast thou any prisoners from my escort?

Hannibal. A few dying lie about—and let them lie—they are Tuscans.   The remainder I saw at a distance, flying, and but one brave man among 15 them—he appeared a Roman—a youth who turned back, though wounded.   They surrounded and dragged him away, spurring his horse with their swords.   These Etrurians measure their courage carefully, and tack it well together before they put 20 it on, but throw it off again with lordly ease.

Marcellus, why think about them? or does aught else disquiet your thoughts?

Marcellus. I have suppressed it long enough. My son—my beloved son!   25

Hannibal. Where is he?   Can it be?   Was he with you?

Marcellus. He would have shared my fate—and has not.   Gods of my country! beneficent through-out life to me, in death surpassingly beneficent: I 30 render you, for the last time, thanks.

P. Scipio Aemilianus, Polybius, Panaetius.

Scipio. Polybius, if you have found me slow in rising to you, if I lifted not up my eyes to salute you on your entrance, do not hold me ungrateful. Proud there is no danger that you will ever call me: 5 this day of all days would least make me so; it shows me the power of the immortal gods, the mutability of fortune, the instability of empire, the feebleness, the nothingness of man. The earth stands motionless; the grass upon it bends 10 and returns, the same to-day as yesterday, the same in this age as in a hundred past; the sky darkens and is serene again; the clouds melt away, but they are clouds another time, and float like triumphal pageants along the heavens. Carthage 15 is fallen, to rise no more! The funereal horns have this hour announced to us that, after eighteen days and eighteen nights of conflagration, her last embers are extinguished.

Polybius. Perhaps, O Æmilianus, I ought not to 20 have come in.

Scipio. Welcome, my friend.

Polybius. While you were speaking, I would by no means interrupt you so idly as to ask you to whom you have been proud, or to whom could you 25 be ungrateful?

Scipio. To him, if to any, whose hand is in mine; to

him on whose shoulder I rest my head, weary with presages and vigils. Collect my thoughts for me, O my friend! the fall of Cathage hath shaken and scattered them. There are moments when, if we are quite contented with ourselves, we never can 5 remount to what we were before.

Polybius. Panætius is absent.

Scipio. Feeling the necessity, at the moment, of utter loneliness, I despatched him toward the city. There may be (yes, even there) some suffer- 10 ings which the Senate would not censure us for assuaging. But behold he returns! We were speaking of you, Panætius!

Panætius. And about what beside? Come, honestly tell me, Polybius, on what are you reflect- 15 ing and meditating with such sedately intense enthusiasm?

Polybius. After the burning of some village, or the overleaping of some garden-wall, to exterminate a few pirates or highwaymen, I have seen the 20 commander's tent thronged with officers; I have heard as many trumpets around him as would have shaken down the places of themselves; I have seen the horses start from the prætorium, as if they would fly from under their trappings, and spurred 25 as if they were to reach the east and west before sunset, that nations might hear of the exploit, and sleep soundly. And now do I behold in solitude, almost in gloom, and in such silence that, unless my voice prevents it, the grasshopper is audible, 30 him who has levelled to the earth the strongest and most populous of cities, the wealthiest and most

formidable of empires. I had seen Rome; I had
seen (what those who never saw never *will* see)
Carthage! I thought I had seen Scipio; it was but
the image of him: here I find him.

5 *Scipio.* There are many hearts that ache this
day; there are many that never will ache more:
hath one man done it? one man's breath? What
air upon the earth, or upon the waters, or in the
void of heaven is lost so quickly? It flies away at
10 the point of an arrow, and returns no more! the
sea-foam stifles it! the tooth of a reptile stops it!
a noxious leaf suppresses it. What are we in our
greatness?—whence rises it? whither tends it?

Merciful gods! may not Rome be what Carthage
15 is? May not those who love her devotedly, those
who will look on her with fondness and affection
after life, see her in such condition as to wish she
were so?

Polybius. One of the heaviest groans over fallen
20 Carthage burst from the breast of Scipio! Who
would believe this tale?

Scipio. Men like my Polybius: others must never
hear it.

Polybius. You have not ridden forth, Æmilianus,
25 to survey the ruins?

Scipio. No, Polybius: since I removed my tent to
avoid the heat from the conflagration, I never have
ridden nor walked nor looked toward them. At
this elevation, and three miles off, the temperature
30 of the season is altered. I do not believe, as those
about me would have persuaded me, that the gods
were visible in the clouds; that thrones of ebony

and gold were scattered in all directions; that
broken chariots, and flaming steeds, and brazen
bridges, had cast their fragments upon the earth;
that eagles and lions, dolphins and tridents, and
other emblems of power and empire, were visible 5
at one moment and at the next had vanished; that
purple and scarlet overspread the mansions of the
gods; that their voices were heard at first con-
fusedly and discordantly; and that the apparition
closed with their high festivals. I could not keep 10
my eyes on the heavens: a crash of arch or of
theatre or of tower, a column of flame rising higher
than they were, or a universal cry as if none until
then had perished, drew them thitherward. Such
were the dismal sights and sounds, a fresh city 15
seemed to have been taken every hour for seven-
teen days. This is the nineteenth since the smoke
arose from the level roofs and from the lofty temples; and thousands died, and tens of thousands
ran in search of death. 20

Calamity moves me; heroism moves me more.
That a nation whose avarice we have so often rep-
rehended should have cast into the furnace gold
and silver, from the insufficiency of brass and iron
for arms; that palaces the most magnificent should 25
have been demolished by the proprietor for their
beams and rafters, in order to build a fleet against
us; that the ropes whereby the slaves hauled them
down to the new harbour should in part be composed of hair, for one lock of which kings would 30
have laid down their diadems; that Asdrubal
should have found equals, his wife none,—my

mind, my very limbs, are unsteady with admiration!

O Liberty! what art thou to the valiant and brave, when thou art thus to the weak and timid?
5 —dearer than life, stronger than death, higher than purest love. Never will I call upon thee where thy name can be profaned, and never shall my soul acknowledge a more exalted Power than thee.

     •   •   •   •   •   •   •

Metellus and Marius.

Metellus. Well met, Caius Marius! My orders are to find instantly a centurion who shall mount the walls; one capable of observation, acute in remark, prompt, calm, active, intrepid. The Numantians are sacrificing to the gods in secrecy; 5 they have sounded the horn once only,—and hoarsely and low and mournfully.

Marius. Was that ladder I see yonder among the caper-bushes and purple lilies, under where the fig-tree grows out of the rampart, left for me? 10

Metellus. Even so, wert thou willing. Wouldst thou mount it?

Marius. Rejoicingly. If none are below or near, may I explore the state of things by entering the city? 15

Metellus. Use thy discretion in that. What seest thou? Wouldst thou leap down? Lift the ladder.

Marius. Are there spikes in it where it sticks in the turf? I should slip else. 20

Metellus. How! bravest of our centurions, art even thou afraid? Seest thou any one by?

Marius. Ay; some hundreds close beneath me.

Metellus. Retire, then. Hasten back; I will protect thy descent. 25

Marius. May I speak, O Metellus, without an offence to discipline?

Metellus. Say.

Marius. Listen! Dost thou not hear?

Metellus. Shame on thee! alight, alight! my shield shall cover thee.

5 *Marius.* There is a murmur like the hum of bees in the bean-field of Cereate; for the sun is hot, and the ground is thirsty. When will it have drunk up for me the blood that has run, and is yet oozing on it, from those fresh bodies!

10 *Metellus.* How! We have not fought for many days; what bodies, then, are fresh ones?

Marius. Close beneath the wall are those of infants and of girls; in the middle of the road are youths, emaciated; some either unwounded or 15 wounded months ago; some on their spears, others on their swords: no few have received in mutual death the last interchange of friendship; their daggers unite them, hilt to hilt, bosom to bosom.

Metellus. Mark rather the living,—what are they 20 about?

Marius. About the sacrifice, which portends them, I conjecture, but little good,—it burns sullenly and slowly. The victim will lie upon the pyre till morning, and still be unconsumed, unless they 25 bring more fuel.

I will leap down and walk on cautiously, and return with tidings, if death should spare me.

Never was any race of mortals so unmilitary as these Numantians: no watch, no stations, no pali-30 sades across the streets.

Metellus. Did they want, then, all the wood for the altar?

Marius. It appears so,—I will return anon.

Metellus. The gods speed thee, my brave, honest Marius!

Marius (*returned*). The ladder should have been better spiked for that slippery ground. I am down 5 again safe, however. Here a man may walk securely, and without picking his steps.

Metellus. Tell me, Caius, what thou sawest.

Marius. The streets of Numantia.

Metellus. Doubtless; but what else?   10

Marius. The temples and markets and places of exercise and fountains.

Metellus. Art thou crazed, centurion? what more? Speak plainly, at once, and briefly.

Marius. I beheld, then, all Numantia.   15

Metellus. Has terror maddened thee? hast thou descried nothing of the inhabitants but those carcasses under the ramparts?

Marius. Those, O Metellus, lie scattered, although not indeed far asunder. The greater part of 20 the soldiers and citizens—of the fathers, husbands, widows, wives, espoused—were assembled together.

Metellus. About the altar?

Marius. Upon it.

Metellus. So busy and earnest in devotion! but 25 how all upon it?

Marius. It blazed under them, and over them, and round about them.

Metellus. Immortal gods! Art thou sane, Caius Marius? Thy visage is scorched: thy speech may 30 wander after such an enterprise; thy shield burns my hand.

Marius. I thought it had cooled again. Why, truly, it seems hot: I now feel it.

Metellus. Wipe off those embers.

Marius. 'Twere better: there will be none oppo· 5 site to shake them upon, for some time.

The funereal horn, that sounded with such feeble- ness, sounded not so from the faint heart of him who blew it. Him I saw; him only of the living. Should I say it? there was another: there was one child whom 10 its parent could not kill, could not part from. She had hidden it in her robe, I suspect; and, when the fire had reached it, either it shrieked or she did. For suddenly a cry pierced through the crackling pinewood, and something of round in figure fell 15 from brand to brand, until it reached the pavement, at the feet of him who had blown the horn. I rushed toward him, for I wanted.to hear the whole story, and felt the pressure of time. Condemn not my weakness, O Cæcilius! I wished an enemy to 20 live an hour longer; for my orders were to explore and bring intelligence. When I gazed on him, in height almost gigantic, I wondered not that the blast of his trumpet was so weak: rather did I wonder that Famine, whose hand had indented 25 every limb and feature, had left him any voice articulate. I rushed toward him, however, ere my eyes had measured either his form or strength. He held the child against me, and staggered under it.

"Behold," he exclaimed, "the glorious ornament 30 of a Roman triumph!"

I stood horror-stricken; when suddenly drops, as of rain, pattered down from the pyre. I looked;

and many were the precious stones, many were the amulets and rings and bracelets, and other barbaric ornaments, unknown to me in form or purpose, that tinkled on the hardened and black branches, from mothers and wives and betrothed maids; and some, 5 too, I can imagine, from robuster arms—things of joyance, won in battle. The crowd of incumbent bodies was so dense and heavy that neither the fire nor the smoke could penetrate upward from among them; and they sank, whole and at once, into the 10 smouldering cavern eaten out below. He at whose neck hung the trumpet felt this, and started.

"There is yet room," he cried, "and there is strength enough yet, both in the element and in me." 15

He extended his withered arms, he thrust forward the gaunt links of his throat, and upon gnarled knees, that smote each other audibly, tottered into the civic fire. It—like some hungry and strangest beast on the innermost wild of Africa, 20 pierced, broken, prostrate, motionless, gazed at by its hunter in the impatience of glory, in the delight of awe—panted once more, and seized him.

I have seen within this hour, O Metellus, what Rome in the cycle of her triumphs will never see, 25 what the Sun in his eternal course can never show her, what the Earth has borne but now, and must never rear again for her, what Victory herself has envied her,—a Numantian.

Metellus. We shall feast to-morrow. Hope, 30 Caius Marius, to become a tribune: trust in fortune.

Marius. Auguries are surer: surest of all is perseverance.

Metellus. I hope the wine has not grown vapid
in my tent: I have kept it waiting, and must now
5 report to Scipio the intelligence of our discovery.
Come after me, Caius.

Marius (alone). The tribune is the discoverer!
the centurion is the scout! Caius Marius must
enter more Numantias. Light-hearted Cæcilius,
10 thou mayest perhaps hereafter, and not with
humbled but with exulting pride, take orders from
this hand. If Scipio's words are fate, and to me
they sound so, the portals of the Capitol may shake
before my chariot, as my horses plunge back at the
15 applauses of the people, and Jove in his high dom-
icile may welcome the citizen of Arpinum.

Lucullus and Cæsar.

Cæsar. Lucius Lucullus, I come to you privately and unattended for reasons which you will know; confiding, I dare not say in your friendship, since no service of mine toward you hath deserved it, but in your generous and disinterested love of peace. 5 Hear me on. Cneius Pompeius, according to the report of my connections in the city, had, on the instant of my leaving it for the province, begun to solicit his dependents to strip me ignominiously of authority. Neither vows nor affinity can bind him. 10 He would degrade the father of his wife; he would humiliate his own children, the unoffending, the unborn; he would poison his own nascent love— at the suggestion of Ambition. Matters are now brought so far that either he or I must submit to a 15 reverse of fortune; since no concession can assuage his malice, divert his envy, or gratify his cupidity. No sooner could I raise myself up, from the consternation and stupefaction into which the certainty of these reports had thrown me, than I began to 20 consider in what manner my own private afflictions might become the least noxious to the republic. Into whose arms, then, could I throw myself more naturally and more securely, to whose bosom could I commit and consign more sacredly the hopes and 25 destinies of our beloved country, than his who laid down power in the midst of its enjoyments, in the vigour of youth, in the pride of triumph, when Dignity solicited, when Friendship urged, entreated, supplicated, and when Liberty herself 5 invited and beckoned to him from the senatorial order and from the curule chair? Betrayed and abandoned by those we had confided in, our next friendship, if ever our hearts receive any, or if any will venture in those places of desolation, flies for-10 ward instinctively to what is most contrary and dissimilar. Cæsar is hence the visitant of Lucullus.

Lucullus. I had always thought Pompeius more moderate and more reserved than you represent him, Caius Julius; and yet I am considered in 15 general, and surely you also will consider me, but little liable to be prepossessed by him.

Cæsar. Unless he may have ingratiated himself with you recently, by the administration of that worthy whom last winter his partisans dragged 20 before the Senate, and forced to assert publicly that you and Cato had instigated a party to circumvent and murder him; and whose carcass, a few days afterward, when it had been announced that he had died by a natural death, was found covered 25 with bruises, stabs, and dislocations.

Lucullus. You bring much to my memory which had quite slipped out of it, and I wonder that it could make such an impression on yours. A proof to me that the interest you take in my behalf began 30 earlier than your delicacy will permit you to acknowledge. You are fatigued, which I ought to have perceived before.

Cæsar. Not at all; the fresh air has given me life and alertness: I feel it upon my cheek even in the room.

Lucullus. After our dinner and sleep, we will spend the remainder of the day on the subject of 5 your visit.

Cæsar. Those Ethiopian slaves of yours shiver with cold upon the mountain here; and truly I myself was not insensible to the change of climate, in the way from Mutina.   10

What white bread! I never found such even at Naples or Capua. This Formian wine (which I prefer to the Chian), how exquisite!

Lucullus. Such is the urbanity of Cæsar, even while he bites his lip with displeasure. How! 15 surely it bleeds! Permit me to examine the cup.

Cæsar. I believe a jewel has fallen out of the rim in the carriage: the gold is rough there.

Lucullus. Marcipor, let me never see that cup again! No answer, I desire. My guest pardons 20 heavier faults. Mind that dinner be prepared for us shortly.

Cæsar. In the meantime, Lucullus, if your health permits it, shall we walk a few paces round the villa? for I have not seen anything of the kind 25 before.

.   .   .   .   .

Lucullus. You are surveying the little lake beside us. It contains no fish, birds never alight on it, the water is extremely pure and cold; the walk round is pleasant, not only because there is 30 always a gentle breeze from it, but because the turf is fine, and the surface of the mountain on this summit is perfectly on a level to a great extent in length—not a trifling advantage to me, who walk often and am weak. I have no alley, no garden, 5 no enclosure; the park is in the vale below, where a brook supplies the ponds, and where my servants are lodged; for here I have only twelve in attendance.

Cæsar. What is that so white, toward the 10 Adriatic?

Lucullus. The Adriatic itself. Turn round and you may descry the Tuscan Sea. Our situation is reported to be among the highest of the Apennines. —Marcipor has made the sign to me that dinner is 15 ready. Pass this way.

.   .   .   .   .   .

This other is my dining-room. You expect the dishes.

Cæsar. I misunderstood,—I fancied——

Lucullus. Repose yourself, and touch with the 20 ebony wand, beside you, the sphinx on either of those obelisks, right or left.

Cæsar. Let me look at them first.

Lucullus. The contrivance was intended for one person, or two at most, desirous of privacy and 25 quiet. The blocks of jasper in my pair, and of porphyry in yours, easily yield in their grooves, each forming one partition. There are four, containing four platforms. The lower holds four dishes, such as sucking forest-boars, venison, 30 hares, tunnies, sturgeons, which you will find within; the upper three, eight each, but diminu-

tive.   The confectionery is brought separately, for
the steam would spoil it, if any should escape.
The melons are in the snow, thirty feet under us:
they came early this morning from a place in the
vicinity of Luni, so that I hope they may be crisp, 5
independently of their coolness.

Cæsar. I wonder not at anything of refined
elegance in Lucullus; but really here Antiochia
and Alexandria seem to have cooked for us, and
magicians to be our attendants.   10

Lucullus. The absence of slaves from our repast
is the luxury, for Marcipor alone enters, and he
only when I press a spring with my foot or wand.
When you desire his appearance, touch that chal-
cedony just before you.

Cæsar. I eat quick and rather plentifully; yet 15
the valetudinarian (excuse my rusticity, for I rejoice at seeing it) appears to equal the traveller in
appetite, and to be contented with one dish.

Lucullus. It is milk: such, with strawberries, 20
which ripen on the Apennines many months in continuance, and some other berries of sharp and
grateful flavour, has been my only diet since my
first residence here.   The state of my health requires it; and the habitude of nearly three months 25
renders this food not only more commodious to my
studies and more conducive to my sleep, but also
more agreeable to my palate than any other.

Cæsar. Returning to Rome or Baiæ, you must
domesticate and tame them.   The cherries you 30
introduced from Pontus are now growing in Cisal-
pine and Transalpine Gaul; and the largest and

best in the world, perhaps, are upon the more
sterile side of Lake Larius.

Lucullus. There are some fruits, and some virtues,
which require a harsh soil and bleak exposure for
5 their perfection.

Cæsar. In such a profusion of viands, and so
savoury, I perceive no odour.

Lucullus. A flue conducts heat through the com-
partments of the obelisks; and, if you look up, you
10 may observe that those gilt roses, between the
astragals in the cornice, are prominent from it half
a span. Here is an aperture in the wall, between
which and the outer is a perpetual current of air.
We are now in the dog-days; and I have never felt
15 in the whole summer more heat than at Rome
in many days of March.

Cæsar. Usually you are attended by troops of
domestics and of dinner-friends, not to mention
the learned and scientific, nor your own family,
20 your attachment to which, from youth upward, is
one of the higher graces in your character. Your
brother was seldom absent from you.

Lucullus. Marcus was coming; but the vehement
heats along the Arno, in which valley he has a
25 property he never saw before, inflamed his blood,
and he now is resting for a few days at Fæsulæ, a
little town destroyed by Sylla within our memory,
who left it only air and water, the best in Tuscany
The health of Marcus, like mine, has been declin-
30 ing for several months: we are running our last
race against each other, and never was I, in youth
along the Tiber, so anxious of first reaching the

goal. I would not outlive him: I should reflect
too painfully on earlier days, and look forward too
despondently on future. As for friends, lampreys
and turbots beget them, and they spawn not amid
the solitude of the Apennines. To dine in company 5
with more than two is a Gaulish and German thing.
I can hardly bring myself to believe that I have
eaten in concert with twenty; so barbarous and
herdlike a practice does it now appear to me—such
an incentive to drink much and talk loosely; not 10
to add, such a necessity to speak loud, which is
clownish and odious in the extreme. On this
mountain summit I hear no noises, no voices, not
even of salutation; we have no flies about us, and
scarcely an insect or reptile.   15

Cæsar. Your amiable son is probably with his
uncle: is he well?

Lucullus. Perfectly. He was indeed with my
brother in his intended visit to me; but Marcus,
unable to accompany him hither, or superintend 20
his studies in the present state of his health, sent
him directly to his Uncle Cato at Tusculum—a
man fitter than either of us to direct his education,
and preferable to any, excepting yourself and
Marcus Tullius, in eloquence and urbanity.   25

Cæsar. Cato is so great that whoever is greater
must be the happiest and first of men.

Lucullus. That any such be still existing, O
Julius, ought to excite no groan from the breast of
a Roman citizen. But perhaps I wrong you; per- 30
haps your mind was forced reluctantly back again,
on your past animosities and contests in the Senate.

Cæsar. I revere him, but cannot love him.

Lucullus. Then, Caius Julius, you groaned with reason; and I would pity rather than reprove you.

5 On the ceiling at which you are looking, there is no gilding, and little painting—a mere trellis of vines bearing grapes, and the heads, shoulders, and arms, rising from the cornice only, of boys and girls climbing up to steal them, and scrambling for 10 them: nothing overhead; no giants tumbling down, no Jupiter thundering, no Mars and Venus caught at mid-day, no river-gods pouring out their urns upon us; for, as I think nothing so insipid as a flat ceiling, I think nothing so absurd as a storied one. 15 Before I was aware, and without my participation, the painter had adorned that of my bed-chamber with a golden shower, bursting from varied and irradiated clouds. On my expostulation, his excuse was that he knew the Danaë of Scopas, in a 20 recumbent posture, was to occupy the centre of the room. The walls, behind the tapestry and pictures, are quite rough. In forty-three days the whole fabric was put together and habitable.

The wine has probably lost its freshness: will 25 you try some other?

Cæsar. Its temperature is exact; its flavour exquisite. Latterly I have never sat long after dinner, and am curious to pass through the other apartments, if you will trust me.

30 *Lucullus.* I attend you.

Cæsar. Lucullus, who is here? What figure is that on the poop of the vessel? Can it be——

Lucullus. The subject was dictated by myself; you gave it.

Cæsar. Oh, how beautifully is the water painted! How vividly the sun strikes against the snows on Taurus! The gray temples and pier-head of 5 Tarsus catch it differently, and the monumental mound on the left is half in shade. In the countenance of those pirates I did not observe such diversity, nor that any boy pulled his father back: I did not indeed mark them or notice them at all. 10

Lucullus. The painter in this fresco, the last work finished, had dissatisfied me in one particular. "That beautiful young face," said I, "appears not to threaten death."

"Lucius," he replied, "if one muscle were 15 moved it were not Cæsar's: beside, he said it jokingly, though resolved."

"I am contented with your apology, Antipho; but what are you doing now? for you never lay down or suspend your pencil, let who will talk and 20 argue. The lines of that smaller face in the distance are the same."

"Not the same," replied he, "nor very different: it smiles, as surely the goddess must have done at the first heroic act of her descendant." 25

Cæsar. In her exultation and impatience to press forward she seems to forget that she is standing at the extremity of the shell, which rises up behind out of the water; and she takes no notice of the terror on the countenance of this Cupid who would 30 detain her, nor of this who is flying off and looking back. The reflection of the shell has given a warmer hue below the knee; a long streak of yellow light in the horizon is on the level of her bosom, some of her hair is almost lost in it; above her head on every side is the pure azure of the heavens.

5   Oh! and you would not have led me up to this? You, among whose primary studies is the most perfect satisfaction of your guests!

Lucullus. In the next apartment are seven or eight other pictures from our history.

10   There are no more: what do you look for?

Cæsar. I find not among the rest any descriptive of your own exploits. Ah, Lucullus! there is no surer way of making them remembered.

This, I presume by the harps in the two corners, 15 is the music-room.

Lucullus. No, indeed; nor can I be said to have one here; for I love best the music of a single instrument, and listen to it willingly at all times, but most willingly while I am reading. At such 20 seasons a voice or even a whisper disturbs me; but music refreshes my brain when I have read long, and strengthens it from the beginning. I find also that if I write anything in poetry (a youthful propensity still remaining), it 25 gives rapidity and variety and brightness to my ideas. On ceasing, I command a fresh measure and instrument, or another voice; which is to the mind like a change of posture, or of air to the body. My health is benefited by the gentle play 30 thus opened to the most delicate of the fibres.

Cæsar. Let me augur that a disorder so tractable may be soon removed. What is it thought to be?

Lucullus. There are they who would surmise and signify, and my physician did not long attempt to persuade me of the contrary, that the ancient realms of Æetes have supplied me with some other plants than the cherry, and such as I should be sorry to 5 see domesticated here in Italy.

Cæsar. The gods forbid! Anticipate better things! The reason of Lucullus is stronger than the medica- ments of Mithridates; but why not use them, too? Let nothing be neglected. You may reasonably hope 10 for many years of life: your mother still enjoys it.

Lucullus. To stand upon one's guard against Death exasperates her malice and protracts our sufferings.

Cæsar. Rightly and gravely said: but your 15 country at this time cannot do well without you.

Lucullus. The bowl of milk, which to-day is pre- sented to me, will shortly be presented to my Manes.

Cæsar. Do you suspect the hand? 20

Lucullus. I will not suspect a Roman: let us con- verse no more about it.

Cæsar. It is the only subject on which I am resolved never to think, as relates to myself. Life may concern us, death not; for in death we 25 neither can act nor reason, we neither can persuade nor command; and our statues are worth more than we are, let them be but wax. Lucius, I will not divine your thoughts; I will not penetrate into your suspicions, nor suggest mine. I am lost in 30 admiration of your magnanimity and forbearance— that your only dissimulation should be upon the guilt of your assassin; that you should leave him power, and create him virtues.

.   .   .   .   .   .

Lucullus. Hear me, and believe me.   I am about to mount higher than triumviral tribunal, or than 5 triumphal car.   They who are under me will turn their faces from me; such are the rites: but not a voice of reproach or of petulance shall be heard, when the trumpets tell our city that the funereal flames are surmounting the mortal spoils of Lucullus.

10   *Cæsar.* Mildest and most equitable of men!   I have been much wronged; would you also wrong me?   Lucius, you have forced from me a tear before the time.   I weep at magnanimity; which no man does who wants it.

15   *Lucullus.* Why cannot you enjoy the command of your province, and the glory of having quelled so many nations?

Cæsar. I cannot bear the superiority of another.

Lucullus. The weakest of women feel so; but 20 even the weakest of them are ashamed to acknowledge it: who hath ever heard any one?   Have *you*, who know them widely and well?   Poetasters and mimes, labouring under such infirmity, put the mask on.   You pursue glory: the pursuit is just and 25 rational; but reflect that statuaries and painters have represented heroes calm and quiescent, not straining and panting like pugilists and gladiators.

From being for ever in action, for ever in contention, and from excelling in them all other mortals, 30 what advantage derive we?   I would not ask what satisfaction, what glory?   The insects have more

activity than ourselves, the beasts more strength,
even inert matter more firmness and stability; the
gods alone more goodness. To the exercise of this
every country lies open; and neither I eastward nor
you westward have found any exhausted by contests 5
for it.

Must we give men blows because they will not
look at us? or chain them to make them hold the
balance evener?

Do not expect to be acknowledged for what you 10
are, much less for what you would be; since no one
can well measure a great man but upon the bier.
There was a time when the most ardent friend to
Alexander of Macedon would have embraced the
partisan for his enthusiasm, who should have com- 15
pared him with Alexander of Pheræ.   It must have
been at a splendid feast, and late at it, when Scipio
should have been raised to an equality with
Romulus, or Cato with Curius.   It has been whispered in my ear, after a speech of Cicero, " If he 20
goes on so, he will tread down the sandal of Marcus Antonius in the long run, and perhaps leave
Hortensius behind."   Officers of mine, speaking
about you, have exclaimed with admiration, " He
fights like Cinna."   Think, Caius Julius (for you 25
have been instructed to think both as a poet and as
a philosopher), that among the hundred hands of
Ambition, to whom we may attribute them more
properly than to Briareus, there is not one which
holds anything firmly.   In the precipitancy of her 30
course, what appears great is small, and what
appears small is great.   Our estimate of men is apt

to be as inaccurate and inexact as that of things, or
more. Wishing to have all on our side, we often
leave those we should keep by us, run after those
we should avoid, and call importunately on others
5 who sit quiet and will not come. We cannot at
once catch the applause of the vulgar and expect
the approbation of the wise. What are parties?
Do men really great ever enter into them? Are
they not ball-courts, where ragged adventurers
10 strip and strive, and where dissolute youths abuse
one another, and challenge and game and wager?
If you and I cannot quite divest ourselves of
infirmities and passions, let us think however that
there is enough in us to be divided into two por-
15 tions, and let us keep the upper undisturbed and
pure. A part of Olympus itself lies in dreariness
and in clouds, variable and stormy; but it is not
the highest: there the gods govern. Your soul is
large enough to embrace your country: all other
20 affection is for less objects, and less men are
capable of it. Abandon, O Cæsar! such thoughts
and wishes as now agitate and propel you: leave
them to mere men of the marsh, to fat hearts and
miry intellects. Fortunate may we call ourselves to
25 have been born in an age so productive of eloquence, so rich in erudition. Neither of us would
be excluded, or hooted at, on canvassing for these
honours. He who can think dispassionately and
deeply as I do, is great as I am; none other. But
30 his opinions are at freedom to diverge from mine, as
mine are from his; and indeed, on recollection, I never
loved those most who thought with me, but those

rather who deemed my sentiments worth discussion, and who corrected me with frankness and affability.

Cæsar. Lucullus, you perhaps have taken the wiser and better part, certainly the pleasanter. I cannot argue with you: I would gladly hear one who 5 could, but you again more gladly. I should think unworthily of you if I thought you capable of yielding or receding. I do not even ask you to keep our conversation long a secret, so greatly does it preponderate in your favour; so much more of gen- 10 tleness, of eloquence, and of argument. I came hither with one soldier, avoiding the cities, and sleeping at the villa of a confidential friend. To-night I sleep in yours, and, if your dinner does not disturb me, shall sleep soundly. You go early to 15 rest, I know.

Lucullus. Not, however, by daylight. Be assured, Caius Julius, that greatly as your discourse afflicts me, no part of it shall escape my lips. If you approach the city with arms, with arms I meet you; 20 then your denouncer and enemy, at present your host and confidant.

Cæsar. I shall conquer you.

Lucullus. That smile would cease upon it: you sigh already. 25

Cæsar. Yes, Lucullus, if I am oppressed I shall overcome my oppressor: I know my army and myself. A sigh escaped me, and many more will follow; but one transport will rise amid them, when, vanquisher of my enemies and avenger of my dig- 30 nity, I press again the hand of Lucullus, mindful of this day.

Tiberius and Vipsania.

Tiberius. Vipsania, my Vipsania, whither art thou walking?

Vipsania. Whom do I see?—my Tiberius?

Tiberius. Ah! no, no, no! but thou seest the
5 father of thy little Drusus. Press him to thy heart the more closely for this meeting, and give him——

Vipsania. Tiberius! the altars, the gods, the destinies, are between us—I will take it from this hand; thus, thus shall he receive it.

10 *Tiberius.* Raise up thy face, my beloved! I must not shed tears. Augustus! Livia! ye shall not extort them from me. Vipsania! I may kiss thy head—for I have saved it. Thou sayest nothing. I have wronged thee; ay?

15 *Vipsania.* Ambition does not see the earth she treads on; the rock and the herbage are of one substance to her. Let me excuse you to my heart, O Tiberius. It has many wants; this is the first and greatest.

20 *Tiberius.* My ambition, I swear by the immortal gods, placed not the bar of severance between us. A stronger hand, the hand that composes Rome and sways the world——

Vipsania. Overawed Tiberius. I know it; Augus-
25 tus willed and commanded it.

Tiberius. And overawed Tiberius! Power bent

Death terrified, a Nero! What is our race, that
any should look down on us and spurn us? Augustus, my benefactor, I have wronged thee! Livia,
my mother, this one cruel deed was thine! To
reign, forsooth, is a lovely thing. O womanly ap- 5
petite! Who would have been before me, though
the palace of Cæsar cracked and split with emperors,
while I, sitting in idleness on a cliff of Rhodes, eyed
the sun as he swang his golden censer athwart the
heavens, or his image as it overstrode the sea? I 10
have it before me; and, though it seems falling on
me, I can smile at it—just as I did from my little
favourite skiff, painted round with the marriage of
Thetis, when the sailors drew their long shaggy hair
across their eyes, many a stadium away from it, to 15
mitigate its effulgence.

These, too, were happy days: days of happiness
like these I could recall and look back upon with
unaching brow.

O land of Greece! Tiberius blesses thee, bidding 20
thee rejoice and flourish.

Why cannot one hour, Vipsania, beauteous and
light as we have led, return?

Vipsania. Tiberius! is it to me that you were
speaking? I would not interrupt you; but I thought 25
I heard my name as you walked away and looked up
toward the East. So silent!

Tiberius. Who dared to call thee? Thou wert
mine before the gods—do they deny it? Was it my
fault—— 30

Vipsania. Since we are separated, and for ever,
O Tiberius, let us think no more on the cause of it.

Let neither of us believe that the other was to blame: so shall separation be less painful.

Tiberius. O mother! and did I not tell thee what she was?—patient in injury, proud in innocence, 5 serene in grief!

Vipsania. Did you say that too? But I think it was so: I had felt little. One vast wave has washed away the impression of smaller from my memory. Could Livia, could your mother, could she who was 10 so kind to me——

Tiberius. The wife of Cæsar did it. But hear me now; hear me: be calm as I am. No weaknesses are such as those of a mother who loves her only son immoderately; and none are so easily worked 15 upon from without. Who knows what impulses she received? She is very, very kind; but she regards me only, and that which at her bidding is to encompass and adorn me. All the weak look after Power, protectress of weakness. Thou art a woman, O 20 Vipsania! is there nothing in thee to excuse my mother? So good she ever was to me! so loving!

Vipsania. I quite forgive her: be tranquil, O Tiberius!

Tiberius. Never can I know peace—never can I 25 pardon—any one. Threaten me with thy exile, thy separation, thy seclusion! Remind me that another climate might endanger thy health!—There death met me and turned me round. Threaten me to take our son from us—our one boy, our helpless little 30 one—him whom we made cry because we kissed him both together! Rememberest thou? Or dost thou not hear? turning thus away from me!

Vipsania. I hear; I hear! Oh cease, my sweet Tiberius! Stamp not upon that stone: my heart lies under it.

Tiberius. Ay, there again death, and more than death, stood before me. Oh, she maddened me, 5 my mother did, she maddened me—she threw me to where I am at one breath. The gods cannot replace me where I was, nor atone to me, nor console me, nor restore my senses. To whom can I fly; to whom can I open my heart; to whom speak plainly? 10 There was upon the earth a man I could converse with, and fear nothing; there was a woman, too, I could love, and fear nothing. What a soldier, what a Roman, was thy father, O my young bride! How could those who never saw him have discoursed so 15 rightly upon virtue!

Vipsania. These words cool my breast like pressing his urn against it. He was brave: shall Tiberius want courage?

Tiberius. My enemies scorn me. I am a garland 20 dropped from a triumphal car, and taken up and looked on for the place I occupied; and tossed away and laughed at. Senators! laugh, laugh! Your merits may be yet rewarded—be of good cheer! Counsel me, in your wisdom, what services 25 I can render you, conscript fathers!

Vipsania. This seems mockery: Tiberius did not smile so, once.

Tiberius. They had not then congratulated me.

Vipsania. On what? 30

Tiberius. And it was not because she was beautiful, as they thought her, and virtuous, as I know

she is; but because the flowers on the altar were to
be tied together by my heart-string. On this they
congratulated me. Their day will come. Their
sons and daughters are what I would wish them to
5 be: worthy to succeed them.

Vipsania. Where is that quietude, that resigna-
tion, that sanctity, that heart of true tenderness?

Tiberius. Where is my love?—my love?

Vipsania. Cry not thus aloud, Tiberius! there is
10 an echo in the place. Soldiers and slaves may
burst in upon us.

Tiberius. And see my tears? There is no echo,
Vipsania; why alarm and shake me so? We are too
high here for the echoes: the city is below us.
15 Methinks it trembles and totters: would it did!
from the marble quays of the Tiber to this rock.
There is a strange buzz and murmur in my brain;
but I should listen so intensely, I should hear the
rattle of its roofs, and shout with joy.

20 *Vipsania.* Calm, O my life! calm this horrible
transport.

Tiberius. Spake I so loud? Did I indeed then and
send my voice after a lost sound, to bring it back;
thou fanciedest it an echo? Wilt not thou laugh
25 with me, as thou wert wont to do, at such an error?
What was I saying to thee, my tender love, when I
commanded—I know not whom—to stand back, on
pain of death? Why starest thou on me in such agony?
Have I hurt thy fingers, child? I loose them; now
30 let me look! Thou turnest thine eyes away from
me. Oh! oh! I hear my crime! Immortal gods! I
cursed then audibly, and before the sun, my mother!

Wolfgang and Henry of Melctal.

Wolfgang. Old man, thou knowest, I doubt not, why thou art brought before me.

Henry. For having been the preserver of Arnold.

Wolfgang. For harbouring and concealing an outlaw. 5

Henry. We all are outlaws.

Wolfgang. What! and confess it?

Henry. Where there is a law for none, what else can we be?

Wolfgang. In consideration of thy age and here- 10 tofore good repute, our emperor in his clemency would remit the sentence passed on thy offence, taking only thy plough and oxen in punishment of disobedience.

Henry. Ploughs and oxen are not instruments 15 and furtherers of disobedience. Why were they taken from me before? Had they never been seized by his Apostolic Majesty, and had not the great man Gessler told me that I, a hoary traitor, should be yoked in place of them, my valiant son had never 20 cursed him and his master.

Wolfgang. I turn pale with horror. Curse the right-hand of the Almighty!

Henry. We were told that Man was his image, long before we ever heard that a dry marten-skin 25 on the shoulder, and a score of cut pebbles on the

head, made any creature his right-hand. This right-
hand does little else than, like children, strip the
image, or, just as they do, break the head of one
against the head of another.

5 *Wolfgang.* What particular hardship couldst thou
complain of?

Henry. Only that, whenever there was a fine
day, my oxen were taken for the emperor's use, and
that my boy was forced to guide them.

10 *Wolfgang.* You had many days left.

Henry. Ay, verily; all winter, from the first of
November to the first of April. While the snow was
from five to three feet deep, I might plough, sow,
and harrow. A green turf was an imperial rescript;
15 and I never saw one in the morning but I met
a soldier at my gate ere noon, and my two poor
beasts were unhoused.

Wolfgang. Factious man! the mildest governments in the world have always exacted this trifle in
20 payment for their protection. Where there is little
coin, there must be labour or its produce; and how
much better is it to give the half, or rather more,
to a lawful master, than the whole to robbers! But
indeed this half is not given: all in right is Cæsar's.
25 Thy Bible says, "Give unto Cæsar that which is Cæsar's, and unto God that which is God's." It does
not say, "Keep anything," which it would doif anything remained. Dost whistle, rogue?

Henry. I cry you mercy, Sir Wolfgang. About
30 the Scripture I dare argue nothing; but about the
thieves,—what thieves have we here? Who is disposed to take away kid or pullet from us? Cannot

we, who are in our own houses, defend them as
well as those who are some hundred miles off?
And, when we cannot, is not our neighbour as ready
to help us as they are? Yet our neighbour would
blush to ask a spoonful of salt for doing it.   5

Wolfgang. Malcontent! what wouldst thou say
if thy master should forbid thee to turn thy barley
into malt, or to plant thy garden, or any plot of it,
with hops?

Henry. I dare not imagine this wrong. To order 10
me how to crop my garden or how to mix my
tankard! To forbid the earth to give its increase in
due season is the heaviest and the rarest curse of
God.   Never, I trust, will our nation be so heart-
less as to endure a like interdict from the wrath of 15
man.

Wolfgang. There is no danger: nevertheless, why
not profit by example, and avoid the chances of mischief? The tortoise, well protected as it is, draws
in its head at the touch of a child.   20

Henry. I will do the same when I am a tortoise.
But we Switzers have our rights and privileges: we
may kill even a hare if we find him in our corn, pro-
vided the land be our freehold.   What nation in
Christendom can say the same, beyond these moun- 25
tains?   We alone are raised to an equality with the
beasts and birds; we alone can leave our country;
we alone pine and perish if we are long absent
from it.

Wolfgang. Is that a privilege?   30

Henry. No, my lord judge: it may be a want, a
weakness; but those who are subject to it are

exempt from many others. Of what are they not capable in defence of their country, to whom she is so dear! We see our parents and children carried to the grave; we lose sight of them, and bear it
5 manfully: on losing sight of our country our hearts melt away.

Wolfgang. Brave men bear it. I left my country to perform my duties in this; and what country is pleasanter than Austria, or more productive of cat-
10 tle and game, of river-fish and capons?

Henry. All men have a birth-place, Sir Wolfgang; but all men have not a country. Nay, there are some who have it not, and who possess almost half a province, with tolls and mills and chases and
15 courts and prisons, and whatever else can make the great contented.

Wolfgang. I should be censurable if I listened longer to such idle and wild discourse. The people of Burgundy are subject to more hardships than
20 thou art; so are those of Swabia and of France. Be obedient and grateful, seeing that others fare worse.

Henry. If my ear is frost-bitten, your worship's toe may be frost-bitten off and never cure me.

Wolfgang. Be comforted and satisfied. The out-
25 lawry of thy son Arnold is reversed, on payment of a slender fine for the proclamation of it, and of another for its annulment, not much heavier.

.   .   .   .

At the same time I am also commanded to de-nounce unto thee that, if ever thou seest thy son
30 again, thou be deprived of eye-sight.

Henry. I am deprived of eye-sight if I do not see

him. Of sun and snows we have seen enough at
seventy. Ho! Arnold! Arnold! help!

Arnold. Father! who hurts thee? Who threatens
thee? Off, gentlemen! Off, strangers! Off, soldiers!
Slaves, miscreants, Austrians, stand off!   5

Wolfgang. Murder in my presence!

Henry. They bleed all five under thy yew-stick—
one is dying—I was faint: I am not so now; fly, in
the name of God! Again, I pray thee, Arnold, if thou
lovest thy father, go, begone! I command thee.   10

Arnold. O God! I heard thy name and was dis-
obedient: my father has commanded and I obey—
forgive me, O my God!

Wolfgang. Seize him, the traitor. Dastards—but
perhaps it may be better to catch him anywhere 15
else. Who would have thought it! fair as morning,
ardent as noon, and terrible as midnight on the
shoals. Thou at least canst not run so fast.

Henry. I hope I cannot.

Wolfgang. Anastasius, call the priest, Reginald 20
Grot, to strengthen him with admonition, and Sigis-
mund Lockhart, the greffier, to translate the sentence into the vulgar tongue; and to read it before
the people, in the name of his Apostolic Majesty
the Emperor and King, Albert, by the grace of God, 25
et cetera; and in the public square to provide that
the sentence be well and duly executed, forthwith.

Henry. Send also for the great man Gessler; tell
him to come and see a sight: he has not many more
such to see. Welcome, good Reginald! welcome 30
too, my worthy master Lockhart! Come, thy band
sits well enough, let it rest; begin.

Lockhart. The instrument must be translated, — a good hour's labour yet, to the ablest clerk.

Henry. Reginald, thou pressest my hand, and sayest nothing. Dost thou turn thy back upon me?
5 Is this thy comfort?

Reginald. There is a Comforter who has given thee strength, and taken mine from me; keep it, good old man; do my tears hurt thee?

Henry. They do, indeed; go home, blessed soul!
10 I never knew thy temper until now. Many have turned away from me before, but none to hide their compassion at my sufferings. What a draught of sight have I taken with my lord judge Wolfgang! It lasts me yet, and will last me for life. O my
15 young eagle, my own Arnold! I shall never see thee more upon the rocks of Uri; never shall I tremble at thy hardihood, nor press thee to my bosom for reproaching thee too much about it. But I shall hear thy carols in the woods of Underwald. Let
20 them be blithe as usual; let them be blither still, for I shall more want pastime, and shall listen for sweet sounds all day long. Do not ask me again, as in the *Lay of the Leap,* whether thou hast given me the heart-ache. I was always in thy songs be-
25 fore they ended, even where spring and summer, even where youth and fair maidens, were discoursed of. Prythee, do not go on so. Above all, I charge thee, Arnold, never say, " O my poor father! art thou blind for me!" I was fancying my Arnold at
30 my side. Foolish old man, with my eyes yet open, and their two balls unbroken. Is this the place? Blow away, boys! the weather is misty; it will

not light: this arrow head is too blunt; have you nothing better? My old eyes are sunken and tough. Ay, that seems sharper: put it just under the piece of mountain-ash; it will soon redden there. Well done, boy, that is right.

Southey and Landor.

. . . . . .

Landor. And now open your *Paradise Lost.*

Southey. Shall we begin with it immediately?—
or shall we listen a little while to the woodlark?
He seems to know what we are about; for there is a
5 sweetness, a variety, and a gravity in his cadences,
befitting the place and theme. Another time we
might afford the whole hour to him.

Landor. The woodlark, the nightingale, and the
ringdove have made me idle for many, even when I
10 had gone into the fields on purpose to gather fresh
materials for composition. A little thing turns me
from one idleness to another. More than once,
when I have taken out my pencil to fix an idea on
paper, the smell of the cedar, held by me uncon-
15 sciously across the nostrils, hath so absorbed the
senses, that what I was about to write down has vanished, altogether and irrecoverably. This vexed
me; for although we may improve a first thought,
and generally do, yet if we lose it, we seldom or never ✓
20 can find another so good to replace it. The latter-
math has less substance, succulence, and fragrance
than the summer crop. I dare not trust my memory
for a moment with anything of my own: it is more
faithful in storing up what is another's. But am I
25 not doing at this instant something like what I
told you about the pencil? If the loss of my own

thoughts vexed me, how much more will the loss of
yours! Now, pray, begin in good earnest.

Southey. Before we pursue the details of a poem,
it is customary to look at it as a whole, and to consider what is the scope and tendency, or what is usu- 5
ally called the moral. But surely it is a silly and
stupid business to talk mainly about the moral of a
poem, unless it professedly be a fable. A good
epic, a good tragedy, a good comedy, will inculcate
several. Homer does not represent the anger of 10
Achilles as being fatal or disastrous to that hero,
which would be what critics call poetical justice;
but he demonstrates in the greater part of the
Iliad the evil effects of arbitrary power, in alienating
an elevated soul from the cause of his country. 15
In the *Odyssea* he shows that every obstacle yields
to constancy and perseverance; yet he does not propose to show it; and there are other morals no less
obvious. Why should the machinery of the longest
poem be drawn out to establish an obvious truth, 20
which a single verse would exhibit more plainly, and
impress more memorably? Both in epic and dramatic poetry it is action, and not moral, that is first
demanded. The feelings and exploits of the principal agent should excite the principal interest. 25
The two greatest of human compositions are here
defective: I mean the *Iliad* and *Paradise Lost.*
Agamemnon is leader of the confederate Greeks
before Troy, to avenge the cause of Menelaus; yet
not only Achilles and Diomed on his side, but Hec- 30
tor and Sarpedon on the opposite, interest us more
than the "king of men," the avenger, or than his

brother, the injured prince, about whom they all are
fighting. In the *Paradise Lost* no principal character seems to have been intended. There is
neither truth nor wit however in saying that Satan
5 is hero of the piece, unless, as is usually the case in
human life, he is the greatest hero who gives the
widest sway to the worst passions. It is Adam who
acts and suffers most, and on whom the conse-
quences have most influence. This constitutes him
10 the main character; although Eve is the more interesting, Satan the more energetic, and on whom the
greater force of poetry is displayed. The Creator
and his angels are quite secondary.

Landor. Must we not confess that every epic
15 hitherto has been defective in plan; and even that
each, until the time of Tasso, was more so than its
predecessor? Such stupendous genius, so much
fancy, so much eloquence, so much vigour of intellect, never were united as in *Paradise Lost.* Yet it
20 is neither so correct nor so varied as the *Iliad*, nor,
however important the action, so interesting. The
moral itself is the reason why it wearies even those
who insist on the necessity of it. Founded on an
event believed by nearly all nations, certainly by all
25 who read the poem, it lays down a principle which
concerns every man's welfare, and a fact which
every man's experience confirms: that great and ir-
remediable misery may arise from apparently small
offences. But will any one say that, in a poetical
30 view, our certainty of moral truth in this position
is an equivalent for the uncertainty *which* of the
agents is what critics call the hero of the piece?

Southey. We are informed in the beginning of the *Iliad* that the poet, or the Muse for him, is about to sing the anger of Achilles, with the disasters it brought down on the Greeks. But these disasters are of brief continuance, and this anger terminates most prosperously. Another fit of anger from another motive, less ungenerous and less selfish, supervenes; and Hector falls because Patroclus had fallen. The son of Peleus, whom the poet in the beginning proposed for his hero, drops suddenly out of sight, abandoning a noble cause from an ignoble resentment. Milton, in regard to the discontinuity of agency, is in the same predicament as Homer.

Let us now take him more in detail. He soon begins to give the learned and less obvious signification to English words. In the sixth line,—

> That on the secret top, etc.

Here *secret* is in the same sense as Virgil's

> *Secretosque* pios, his dantem jura Catonem.

Would it not have been better to omit the fourth and fifth verses, as encumbrances, and deadeners of the harmony; and for the same reason, the fourteenth, fifteenth, and sixteenth?

> That with no middle flight intends to soar
> Above the Aonian mount, while it pursues
> ✻ Things unattempted yet in prose or rhyme.

Landor. Certainly much better: for the harmony of the sentence is complete without them, and they make it gasp for breath. Supposing the fact to be

true, the mention of it is unnecessary and un-
poetical. Little does it become Milton to run in
debt with Ariosto for his

> Cose non dette mai nè in prosa o in rima.

5 Prosaic enough in a rhymed romance, for such is the
Orlando with all its spirit and all its beauty, and far
beneath the dignity of the epic.

Southey. Beside, it interrupts the intensity of
the poet's aspiration in the words,—

10 > And chiefly thou, O Spirit!

Again: I would rather see omitted the five which
follow that beautiful line,—

> Dovelike satst brooding on the vast abyss.

Landor. The ear, however accustomed to the
15 rhythm of these sentences, is relieved of a burden
by rejecting them; and they are not wanted for
anything they convey.

Southey. I am sorry that Milton (v. 34) did not
always keep separate the sublime Satan and " the
20 infernal Serpent." The thirty-eighth verse is the
first hendecasyllabic in the poem. It is much to be
regretted, I think, that he admits this metre into
epic poetry. It is often very efficient in the dramatic, at least in Shakspeare, but hardly ever in
25 Milton. He indulges in it much less fluently in the
Paradise Lost than in the *Paradise Regained.* In
the seventy-third verse he tells us that the rebellious angels are

> As far removed from God and light of heaven
30 > As from the centre thrice to the utmost pole.

Not very far for creatures who could have measured all that distance, and a much greater, by a single act of the will.

V. 188 ends with the word *repair;* 191 with *despair.*

335.   Nor did they not perceive the evil plight   5
    In which they were.

Landor. We are oftener in such *evil plight* of floundering in the prosaic slough about your neighbourhood than in Bunhill Fields.

360.   And Powers that erst in heaven sat on thrones.   10

Excuse my asking why you, and indeed most poets in most places, make a monosyllable of *heaven!* I observe you treat *spirit* in the same manner; and although not *peril,* yet *perilous.* I would not insist at all times on an iambic foot, neither would I de- 15 prive these words of their right to a participation in it.

Southey. I have seized all fair opportunities of introducing the tribrachys, and these are the words that most easily afford one. I have turned over the 20 leaves as far as verse 584, where I wish he had written *Damascus* (as he does elsewhere) for *Damasco,* which never was the English appellation. Beside, he sinks the last vowel in Meröe in *Paradise Regained,* which follows; and should consistently 25 have done the same in Damasco, following the practice of the Italian poets, which certainly is better than leaving the vowels open and gaping at one another.

549.   Anon they move   30
    In perfect phalanx to the Dorian mood.

Thousands of years before there were phalanxes, schools of music, or Dorians.

Landor. Never mind the Dorians, but look at Satan:—

5   571.   And now his heart
            Distends with pride, and, hardening in his strength,
            Glories!

What an admirable pause is here! I wish he had not ended one verse with "*his* heart," and the next
10 with "*his* strength."

.   .   .   .   .

Southey. The fourth book contains several imper-fections. The six verses after 165 efface the de-lightful impression we had just received.

      181.   At one slight *bound* high overleapt all *bound.*

15 Such a play on words, so grave a pun, is unpardon-able: and such a prodigious leap is ill represented by the feat of a wolf in a sheepfold; and still worse by

      188.   A thief bent to unhoard the *cash*
20   Of some rich burgher, whose substantial doors,
            Cross-barr'd and bolted fast, fear no assault,
            In at the window climbs, or o'er the tiles.

Landor. This "in at the window" is very unlike the "bound high above all bound" and *climbing*
25 "o'er the tiles" is the practice of a more deliberate burglar.

      193.   So since into his church lewd hirelings climb.

I must leave the lewd hirelings where I find

them: they are too many for me. I would gladly
have seen omitted all between verses 165 and 205.

   Southey.

  252.   Betwixt them lawns or level downs, and flocks
             Grazing the tender herb.

There had not yet been time for flocks, or even for 5
one flock.

  Landor. At verse 297 commences a series of
verses so harmonious that my ear is impatient of
any other poetry for several days after I have read
them. I mean those which begin,—   10

      For contemplation he and valour formed,
      For softness she and sweet attractive grace;

and ending with,—

      And sweet, reluctant, amorous delay.

  Southey. Here, indeed, is the triumph of our 15
language, and I should say of our poetry, if, in
your preference of Shakspeare, you could endure
my saying it. But, since we seek faults rather
than beauties this morning, tell me whether you
are quite contented with,—   20

      She, as a veil, down to the slender waist
      Her unadornèd golden tresses wore,
      Dishevell'd, but in wanton ringlets waved
      As the vine curls her tendrils; *which implied*
      Subjection, but required with gentle sway,   25
      And by her yielded, by him best received.

  Landor. Stopping there, you break the link of
harmony just above the richest jewel that poetry
ever wore:—

Yielded with coy submission, modest pride,
And sweet, reluctant, amorous delay.

I would rather have written these two lines than all the poetry that has been written since Milton's 5 time in all the regions of the earth. We shall see again things equal in their way to the best of them; but here the sweetest of images and sentiments is seized and carried far away from all pursuers.

.   .   .   .   .

Southey. We open the twelfth book: we see land 10 at last.

Landor. Yes, and dry land too. Happily the twelfth is the shortest. In a continuation of six hundred and twenty-five flat verses, we are prepared for our passage over several such deserts 15 of almost equal extent, and still more frequent, in *Paradise Regained.* But, at the close of the poem now under our examination, there is a brief union of the sublime and the pathetic for about twenty lines, beginning with "All in bright array." 20 We are comforted by the thought that Providence had not abandoned our first parents, but was still their guide; that, although they had lost Paradise, they were not debarred from Eden; that, although the angel had left them solitary and sor-25 rowing, he left them "yet in peace." The termination is proper and complete.

In Johnson's estimate I do not perceive the unfairness of which many have complained. Among his first observations is this: " Scarcely any recital 30 is wished shorter for the sake of quickening the

main action." This is untrue: were it true, why
remark, as he does subsequently, that the poem is
mostly read as a duty, not as a pleasure. I think it
unnecessary to say a word on the moral or the subject; for it requires no genius to select a grand 5
one. The heaviest poems may be appended to the
loftiest themes. Andreini and others, whom Milton
turned over and tossed aside, are evidences. It
requires a large stock of patience to travel through
Vida; and we slacken in our march, although ac- 10
companied with the livelier sing-song of Sannazar.
Let any reader, who is not by many degrees more
pious than poetical, be asked whether he felt a
very great interest in the greatest actors of *Paradise Lost*, in what is either said or done by the 15
angels or the Creator; and whether the humblest
and weakest does not most attract him. Johnson's
remarks on the allegory of Milton are just and
wise; so are those on the non-materiality or non-
immateriality of Satan. These faults might have 20
been easily avoided; but Milton, with all his
strength, chose rather to make antiquity his shield-
bearer, and to come forward under a protection
which he might proudly have disdained.

Southey. You will not countenance the critic, nor 25
Dryden whom he quotes, in saying that Milton
"saw Nature through the spectacles of books"?

Landor. Unhappily, both he and Dryden saw
Nature from between the houses of Fleet Street.
If ever there was a poet who knew her well, and 30
described her in all her loveliness, it was Milton.
In the *Paradise Lost* how profuse in his descrip-

tions, as became the time and place! In the
Allegro and *Penseroso* how exquisite and select!
Johnson asks, "What Englishman can take
delight in transcribing passages which, if they
5 lessen the reputation of Milton, diminish in some
degree the honour of our country!" I hope the
honour of our country will always rest on truth and
justice. It is not by concealing what is wrong
that anything right can be accomplished. There
10 is no pleasure in transcribing such passages; but
there is great utility. Inferior writers exercise no
interest, attract no notice, and serve no purpose.
Johnson has himself done great good by exposing
great faults in great authors. His criticism on
15 Milton's highest work is the most valuable of all
his writings. He seldom is erroneous in his cen-
sures; but he never is sufficiently excited to admiration of what is purest and highest in poetry.
He has this in common with common minds (from
20 which, however, his own is otherwise far remote),
to be pleased with what is nearly on a level with
him, and to drink as contentedly a heady beverage, with its discoloured froth, as what is of the
best vintage. He is morbid, not only in his weak-
25 ness, but in his strength. There is much to pardon, much to pity, much to respect, and no little
to admire, in him.

After I have been reading the *Paradise Lost*,
I can take up no other poet with satisfaction. I
30 seem to have left the music of Handel for the
music of the streets, or at best for drums and fifes.
Although in Shakspeare there are occasional

bursts of harmony no less sublime; yet, if there
were many such in continuation, it would be hurt-
ful, not only in comedy, but also in tragedy. The
greater part should be equable and conversational.
For, if the excitement were the same at the begin- 5
ning, the middle, and the end; if consequently
(as must be the case) the language and versifica-
tion were equally elevated throughout,—any long
poem would be a bad one, and, worst of all, a
drama. In our English heroic verse, such as 10
Milton has composed it, there is a much greater
variety of feet, of movement, of musical notes
and bars, than in the Greek heroic; and the final
sounds are incomparably more diversified. My
predilection in youth was on the side of Homer; 15
for I had read the *Iliad* twice, and the *Odyssea* once,
before the *Paradise Lost*. Averse as I am to everything relating to theology, and especially to the
view of it thrown open by this poem, I recur to it
incessantly as the noblest specimen in the world of 20
eloquence, harmony, and genius.

Southey. Learned and sensible men are of opinion
that the *Paradise Lost* should have ended with
the words, " Providence their guide." It might
very well have ended there; but we are unwilling 25
to lose sight all at once of our first parents. Only
one more glimpse is allowed us: we are thankful
for it. We have seen the natural tears they
dropped; we have seen that they wiped them *soon*.
And why was it? Not because the world was all 30
before them; but because there still remained for
them, under the guidance of Providence, not in-

deed the delights of Paradise, now lost for ever, but the genial clime and calm repose of Eden.

Landor. It has been the practice in late years to supplant one dynasty by another, political and 5 poetical. Within our own memory, no man had ever existed who preferred Lucretius on the whole to Virgil, or Dante to Homer. But the great Florentine, in these days, is extolled high above the Grecian and Milton. Few, I believe, have 10 studied him more attentively or with more delight than I have; but beside the prodigious dispro-portion of the bad to the good, there are funda-mental defects which there are not in either of the other two. In the *Divina Commedia* the charac-15 ters are without any bond of union, any field of action, any definite aim. There is no central light above the Bolge; and we are chilled in Paradise even at the side of Beatrice.

Southey. Some poetical Perillus must surely have 20 invented the *terza rima*. I feel in reading it as a school-boy feels when he is beaten over the head with a bolster.

Landor. We shall hardly be in time for dinner. What should we have been if we had repeated with 25 just eulogies all the noble things in the poem we have been reading?

Southey. They would never have weaned you from the *Mighty Mother* who placed her turreted crown on the head of Shakspeare.

30 *Landor.* A rib of Shakspeare would have made a Milton; the same portion of Milton, all poets born ever since.

Andrew Marvel and Bishop Parker.

Parker. Most happy am I to encounter you, Mr. Marvel. It is some time, I think, since we met. May I take the liberty of inquiring what brought you into such a lonely quarter as Bunhill Fields?

Marvel. My lord, I return at this instant from visiting an old friend of ours, hard by, in Artillery Walk; who, you will be happy to hear, bears his blindness and asthma with truly Christian courage.

Parker. And pray, who may that old friend be, Mr. Marvel?

Marvel. Honest John Milton.

Parker. The same gentleman whose ingenious poem, on our first parents, you praised in some elegant verses prefixed to it?

Marvel. The same who likewise, on many occasions, merited and obtained your lordship's approbation.

Parker. I am happy to understand that no harsh measures were taken against him, on the return of our most gracious sovereign. And it occurs to me that you, Mr. Marvel, were earnest in his behalf. Indeed, I myself might have stirred upon it, had Mr. Milton solicited me in the hour of need.

Marvel. He is grateful to the friends who consulted at the same time his dignity and his safety; but gratitude can never be expected to grow on a

soil hardened by solicitation. Those who are the
most ambitious of power are often the least ambitious of glory. It requires but little sagacity to
foresee that a name will become invested with eter-
5 nal brightness by belonging to a benefactor of
Milton. *I might have served him!* is not always the
soliloquy of late compassion or of virtuous repent-
ance: it is frequently the cry of blind and impo-
tent and wounded pride, angry at itself for having
10 neglected a good bargain, a rich reversion. Believe me, my lord bishop, there are few whom God
has promoted to serve the truly great. They are
never to be superseded, nor are their names to be
obliterated in earth or heaven. Were I to trust
15 my observation rather than my feelings, I
should believe that friendship is only a state of
transition to enmity. The wise, the excellent in
honour and integrity, whom it was once our ambition to converse with, soon appear in our sight no
20 higher than the ordinary class of our acquaintance;
then become fit objects to set our own slender
wits against, to contend with, to interrogate, to
subject to the arbitration, not of their equals, but
of ours; and, lastly,—what indeed is less injustice
25 and less indignity,—to neglect, abandon, and dis-
own.

Parker. I never have doubted that Mr. Milton is
a learned man—indeed, he has proven it; and there
are many who, like yourself, see considerable merit
30 in his poems. I confess that I am an indifferent
judge in these matters; and I can only hope that he
has now corrected what is erroneous in his doctrines.

Marvel. Latterly, he hath never changed a jot, in acting or thinking.

Parker. Wherein I hold him blamable, well aware as I am that never to change is thought an indication of rectitude and wisdom. But if everything in this 5 world is progressive; if everything is defective; if our growth, if our faculties, are obvious and certain signs of it—then surely we should and must be different in different ages and conditions. Consciousness of error is, to a certain extent, a consciousness 10 of understanding; and correction of error is the plainest proof of energy and mastery.

Marvel. No proof of the kind is necessary to my friend; and it was not always that your lordship looked down on him so magisterially in reprehen- 15 sion, or delivered a sentence from so commanding an elevation. I, who indeed am but a humble man, am apt to question my judgment where it differs from his. I am appalled by any supercilious glance at him, and disgusted by any austerity ill assorted 20 with the generosity of his mind. When I consider what pure delight we have derived from it, what treasures of wisdom it has conveyed to us, I find him supremely worthy of my gratitude, love, and veneration; and the neglect in which I now dis- 25 cover him leaves me only the more room for the free effusion of these sentiments. How shallow in comparison is everything else around us, trickling and dimpling in the pleasure-grounds of our literature! If we are to build our summer-houses against 30 ruined temples, let us at least abstain from ruining them for the purpose.

Parker. Nay, nay, Mr. Marvel! so much warmth is uncalled for.

Marvel. Is there anything offensive to your lordship in my expressions?

5 *Parker.* I am not aware that there is. But let us generalise a little; for we are prone to be touchy and testy in favour of our intimates.

Marvel. I believe, my lord, this fault, or sin, or whatsoever it may be designated, is among the few 10 that are wearing fast away.

. . . . .

Parker. You will find your opinions discountenanced by both our universities.

Marvel. I do not want anybody to corroborate my opinions. They keep themselves up by their own 15 weight and consistency. Cambridge on one side and Oxford on the other could lend me no effectual support; and my skiff shall never be impeded by the sedges of Cam, nor grate on the gravel of Isis.

Parker. Mr. Marvel, the path of what we fondly 20 call patriotism is highly perilous. Courts at least are safe.

Marvel. I would rather stand on the ridge of Etna than lower my head in the Grotto del Cane. By the one I may share the fate of a philosopher; 25 by the other I must suffer the death of a cur.

Parker. We are all of us dust and ashes.

Marvel. True, my lord; but in some we recognise the dust of gold and the ashes of the phœnix; in others, the dust of the gateway and the ashes of 30 turf and stubble. With the greatest rulers upon earth, head and crown drop together, and are overlooked. It is true, we read of them in history; but we also read in history of crocodiles and hyænas. With great writers, whether in poetry or prose, what falls away is scarcely more or other than a vesture. The features of the man are imprinted 5 on his works; and more lamps burn over them, and more religiously, than are lighted in temples or churches. Milton, and men like him, bring their own incense, kindle it with their own fire, and leave it unconsumed and unconsumable; and their music, 10 by day and by night, swells along a vault commensurate with the vault of heaven.

Parker. Mr. Marvel, I am admiring the extremely fine lace of your cravat.

Marvel. It cost me less than lawn would have 15 done; and it wins me a reflection. Very few can think that man a great man whom they have been accustomed to meet dressed exactly like themselves; more especially if they happen to find him, not in park, forest, or chase, but warming his limbs 20 by the reflected heat of the bricks in Artillery Walk. In England, a man becomes a great man by living in the middle of a great field; in Italy, by living in a walled city; in France, by living in a courtyard: no matter what lives they lead there. 25

Parker. I am afraid, Mr. Marvel, there is some slight bitterness in your observation.

Marvel. Bitterness, it may be, from the bruised laurel of Milton.

What falsehoods will not men put on, if they can 30 only pad them with a little piety! And how few will expose their whole faces, from a fear of being frost-bitten by poverty! But Milton was among the few.

Parker. Already have we had our Deluge: we are now once more upon dry land again, and we behold 5 the same creation as rejoiced us formerly. Our late gloomy and turbulent times are passed for ever.

Marvel. Perhaps they are, if anything is for ever; but the sparing Deluge may peradventure be commuted for unsparing Fire, as we are threatened. 10 The arrogant, the privileged, the stiff upholders of established wrong, the deaf opponents of equitable reformation, the lazy consumers of ill-requited industry, the fraudulent who, unable to stop the course of the sun, pervert the direction of the 15 gnomon—all these, peradventure, may be gradually consumed by the process of silent contempt, or suddenly scattered by the tempest of popular indignation. As we see in masquerades the real judge and the real soldier stopped and mocked by the 20 fictitious, so do we see in the carnival of to-day the real man of dignity hustled, shoved aside, and derided by those who are invested with the semblance by the milliners of the court. The populace is taught to respect this livery alone, and 25 is proud of being permitted to look through the grating at such ephemeral frippery. And yet false gems and false metals have never been valued above real ones. Until our people alter these notions; until they estimate the wise and virtuous 30 above the silly and profligate, the man of genius above the man of title; until they hold the knave and cheat of·St. James's as low as the knave and cheat of St. Giles's—they are fitter for the slave-market than for any other station.

Parker. You would have no distinctions, I fear.

Marvel. On the contrary, I would have greater than exist at present. You cannot blot or burn out 5 an ancient name; you cannot annihilate past ser-vices; you cannot subtract one single hour from eternity, nor wither one leaf on his brow who hath entered into it. Sweep away from before me the soft grubs of yesterday's formation, generated by 10 the sickliness of the plant they feed upon; sweep them away unsparingly—then will you clearly see distinctions, and easily count the men who have attained them worthily.

Parker.. In a want of respect to established power 15 and principles originated most of the calamities we have latterly undergone.

Marvel. Say rather, in the averseness of that power and the inadequacy of those principles to resist the encroachment of injustice; say rather, 20 on their tendency to distort the poor creatures swaddled up in them; add, moreover, the reluctance of the old women who rock and dandle them to change their habiliments for fresh and wholesome ones. A man will break the windows of his own 25 house, that he may not perish by foul air within; now, whether is he, or those who bolted the door on him, to blame for it? If he is called mad or inconsiderate, it is only by those who are ignorant of the cause and insensible of the urgency. I 30 declare I am rejoiced at seeing a gentleman, whose ancestors have signally served their country, treated

with deference and respect; because it evinces a
sense of justice and of gratitude in the people, and
because it may incite a few others, whose ambition
would take another course, to desire the same.
5 Different is my sentence, when he who has not
performed the action claims more honour than he
who performed it, and thinks himself the worthier
if twenty are between them than if there be one or
none. Still less accordant is it with my principles,
10 and less reducible to my comprehension, that they
who devised the ruin of cities and societies should
be exhibited as deserving much higher distinction
than they who have corrected the hearts and
enlarged the intellects, and have performed it not
15 only without the hope of reward, but almost with
the certainty of persecution.

Parker. Ever too hard upon great men, Mr.
Marvel!

Marvel. Little men in lofty places, who throw
20 long shadows because our sun is setting,—the man
so little and the places so lofty, that, casting my
pebble, I only show where they stand. They would
be less contented with themselves, if they had
obtained their preferment honestly. Luck and
25 dexterity always give more pleasure than intellect
and knowledge; because they fill up what they fall
on to the brim at once, and people run to them
with acclamations at the splash. Wisdom is reserved and noiseless, contented with hard earn-
30 ings, and daily letting go some early acquisition,
to make room for better specimens. But great
is the exultation of a worthless man, when he

receives, for the chips and raspings of his Bridewell logwood, a richer reward than the best and
wisest for extensive tracts of well-cleared truths;
when he who has sold his country——

Parker. Forbear, forbear, good Mr. Marvel!   5

Marvel. When such is higher in estimation than
he who would have saved it; when his emptiness is
heard above the voice that hath shaken Fanati-
cism in her central shrine, that hath bowed down
tyrants to the scaffold, that hath raised up nations 10
from the dust, that alone hath been found worthy
to celebrate, as angels do, creating and redeeming
Love, and to precede with its solitary sound the
trumpet that will call us to our doom.

Parker. I am unwilling to feign ignorance of the 15
gentleman you designate; but really now you would
make a very Homer of him.

Marvel. It appears to me that Homer is to Milton
what a harp is to an organ, though a harp under the
hand of Apollo.   20

Parker. I have always done him justice; I have
always called him a learned man.

Marvel. Call him henceforward the most glorious
one that ever existed upon earth.   If two—Bacon
and Shakspeare—have equalled him in diversity and 25
intensity of power, did either of these spring away
with such resolution from the sublimest heights of
genius, to liberate and illuminate with patient labour
the manacled human race?   And what is his recompense?   The same recompense as all men like him 30
have received, and will receive for ages.   Persecution follows righteousness; the Scorpion is next

in succession to Libra. The fool, however, who
ventures to detract from Milton's genius, in the
night which now appears to close on him, will,
when the dawn has opened on his dull ferocity, be
5 ready to bite off a limb, if he might thereby limp
away from the trap he has prowled into. Among
the gentler, the better, and the wiser, few have
entered yet the awful structure of his mind; few
comprehend, few are willing to contemplate, its
10 vastness. Politics now occupy scarcely a closet in
it. We seldom are inclined to converse on them;
and, when we do, it is jocosely rather than austerely.
For even the bitterest berries grow less acrid when
they have been hanging long on the tree.

.   .   .   .   .

15 *Parker.* Dear me! what a memory you possess,
good Mr. Marvel! You pronounce Latin verses
charmingly. I wish you would go on to the end of
the book.

Marvel. Permit to go on a shorter distance,—to
20 the conclusion of my remarks. As popery caused
the violence of the Reformers, so did prelaty (the
same thing under another name) the violence of the
Presbyterians and Anabaptists. She treated them
inhumanly: she reduced to poverty, she exiled,
25 she maimed, she mutilated, she stabbed, she shot,
she hanged, those who followed Christ in the narrow and quiet lane, rather than along the dust of
the market-road, and who conversed with him
rather in the cottage than the tollbooth. She
30 would have nothing pass unless through her hands;
and she imposed a heavy and intolerable tax on the

necessaries both of physical and of spiritual life. This baronial privilege our Parliament would have suppressed; the King rose against the suppression, and broke his knuckles in the cogs of the mill.   5

Parker. Sad times, Mr. Marvel, sad times! It fills me with heaviness to hear of them.

Marvel. Low places are foggy first; days of sadness wet the people to the skin; they hang loosely for some time upon the ermine, but at last they 10 penetrate it, and cause it to be thrown off. I do not like to hear a man cry out with pain; but I would rather hear one than twenty. Sorrow is the growth of all seasons; we had much, however, to relieve it. Never did our England, since she first 15 emerged from the ocean, rise so high above surrounding nations. The rivalry of Holland, the pride of Spain, the insolence of France, were thrust back by one finger each; yet those countries were then more powerful than they had ever been. 20 The sword of Cromwell was preceded by the mace of Milton; by that mace which, when Oliver had rendered his account, opened to our contemplation the garden-gate of Paradise. And there were some around not unworthy to enter with him. In the 25 compass of sixteen centuries, you will not number on the whole earth so many wise and admirable men as you could have found united in that single day, when England showed her true magnitude and solved the question, *Which is most, one or a million?* 30 There were giants in those days; but giants who feared God, and not who fought against him. Less

men, it appears, are braver. They show him a legal
writ of ejectment, seize upon his house, and riot-
ously carouse therein. But the morning must
come; and heaviness, we know, cometh in the
5 morning.

Parker. Wide is the difference between carousal
and austerity. Your friend miscalculated the steps
to fortune, in which, as we all are the architects of
our own, if we omit the insertion of one or two, the
10 rest are useless in furthering our ascent. He was
too passionate, Mr. Marvel, he was indeed.

Marvel. Superficial men have no absorbing passion: there are no whirlpools in a shallow. I have
often been amused at thinking in what estimation
15 the greatest of mankind were holden by their contemporaries. Not even the most sagacious and
prudent one could discover much of them, or could
prognosticate their future course in the infinity of
space! Men like ourselves are permitted to stand
20 near, and indeed in the very presence of, Milton.
What do they see?—dark clothes, gray hair, and
sightless eyes! Other men have better things:
other men, therefore, are nobler! The stars themselves are only bright by distance; go close, and all
25 is earthy. But vapours illuminate these: from the
breath and from the countenance of God comes
light on worlds higher than they,—worlds to which
he has given the forms and names of Shakspeare
and of Milton.

30 *Parker.* After all, I doubt whether much of his
doctrine is remaining in the public mind.

Marvel. Others are not inclined to remember

all that we remember, and will not attend to us if we propose to tell them half. Water will take up but a certain quantity of salt, even of the finest and purest. If the short memories of men are to be quoted against the excellence of instruction, your 5 lordship would never have censured them from the pulpit for forgetting what was delivered by their Saviour. It is much, my lord bishop, that you allow my friend even the pittance of praise you have bestowed; for, if you will permit me to ex- 10 press my sentiments in verse, which I am in the habit of doing, I would say—

> Men like the ancient kalends, nones, and ides,
> Are reckoned backward, and the first stand last.

I am confident that Milton is heedless of how 15 little weight he is held by those who are of none; and that he never looks toward those somewhat more eminent, between whom and himself there have crept the waters of oblivion. As the pearl ripens in the obscurity of its shell, so ripens in the 20 tomb all the fame that is truly precious. In fame he will be happier than in friendship. Were it possible that one among the faithful of the angels could have suffered wounds and dissolution in his conflict with the false, I should scarcely feel 25 greater awe at discovering on some bleak mountain the bones of this our mighty defender, once shining in celestial panoply, once glowing at the trumpet-blast of God, but not proof against the desperate and the damned, than I have felt at entering the 30 humble abode of Milton, whose spirit already reaches heaven, yet whose corporeal frame hath no quiet or safe resting-place here below. And shall not I, who loved him early, have the lonely and sad privilege to love him still? Or shall fidelity to power 5 be a virtue, and fidelity to tribulation an offence?

Parker. We may best show our fidelity by our discretion. It becomes my station, and suits my principles, to defend the English Constitution, both in Church and State.

10 *Marvel.* You highly praised the *Defence of the English People;* you called it a masterly piece of rhetoric and ratiocination.

Parker. I might have admired the subtilty of it, and have praised the Latinity.

15 *Marvel.* Less reasonably. But his godlike mind shines gloriously throughout his work; only perhaps we look the more intently at it for the cloud it penetrates. Those who think we have enough of his poetry still regret that we possess too little of 20 his prose, and wish especially for more of his historical compositions. Davila and Bacon——

Parker. You mean Lord Verulam.

Marvel. That idle title was indeed thrown over his shoulders; but the trapping was unlikely to rest 25 long upon a creature of such proud paces. He and Davila are the only men of high genius among the moderns who have attempted it; and the greater of them has failed. He wanted honesty, he perverted facts, he courted favour: the present in his 30 eyes was larger than the future.

Parker. The Italians, who far excel us in the writing of history, are farther behind the ancients.

Marvel. True enough.   From Guicciardini and
Machiavelli, the most celebrated of them, we
acquire a vast quantity of trivial information.
There is about them a sawdust which absorbs much
blood and impurity, and of which the level surface 5
is dry; but no traces by what agency rose such
magnificent cities above the hovels of France and
Germany,—none

Ut fortis Etruria crevit,

or, on the contrary, how the mistress of the world 10
sank in the ordure of her priesthood.

Scilicet et rerum facta est nequissima Roma.

We are captivated by no charms of description, we
are detained by no peculiarities of character: we
hear a clamorous scuffle in the street, and we close 15
the door.   How different the historians of antiquity!   We read Sallust, and always are incited by
the desire of reading on, although we are surrounded by conspirators and barbarians; we read
Livy, until we imagine we are standing in an august 20
pantheon, covered with altars and standards, over
which are the four fatal letters that spellbound all
mankind.*   We step forth again among the modern Italians: here we find plenty of rogues, plenty
of receipts for making more; and little else.   In 25
the best passages, we come upon a crowd of dark
reflections, which scarcely a glimmer of glory
pierces through; and we stare at the tenuity of the
spectres, but never at their altitude.

Give me the poetical mind, the mind poetical in 30

*S. P. Q. R.

all things; give me the poetical heart, the heart of
hope and confidence, that beats the more strongly
and resolutely under the good thrown down, and
raises up fabric after fabric on the same founda-
5 tion.

Parker. At your time of life, Mr. Marvel?

Marvel. At mine, my lord bishop! I have lived
with Milton. Such creative and redeeming spirits
are like kindly and renovating Nature. Volcano
10 comes after volcano; yet covereth she with herbage
and foliage, with vine and olive, and with whatever else refreshes and gladdens her the Earth that
has been gasping under the exhaustion of her
throes.

15 *Parker.* He has given us such a description of
Eve's beauty as appears to me somewhat too pic-
torial, too luxuriant, too suggestive, too—I know
not what.

Marvel. The sight of beauty, in her purity and
20 beatitude, turns us from all unrighteousness, and
is death to sin.

Parker. Before we part, my good Mr. Marvel,
let me assure you that we part in amity, and that
I bear no resentment in my breast against your
25 friend. I am patient of Mr. Milton; I am more
than patient,—I am indulgent, seeing that his influence on society is past.

Marvel. Past it is, indeed. What a deplorable
thing is it that folly should so constantly have
30 power over wisdom, and wisdom so intermittently
over folly! But we live morally, as we used to live
politically, under a representative system; and the

majority (to employ a phrase of people at elections) carries the day.

Parker. Let us piously hope, Mr. Marvel, that God in his good time may turn Mr. Milton from the error of his ways, and incline his heart to re- 5 pentance, and that so he may finally be prepared for death.

Marvel. The wicked can never be prepared for it; the good always are. What is the preparation which so many ruffled wrists point out?—to gabble 10 over prayer and praise and confession and contrition. My lord, heaven is not to be won by short hard work at the last, as some of us take a degree at the university, after much irregularity and negligence. I prefer a steady pace from the outset to 15 the end; coming in cool, and dismounting quietly. Instead of which, I have known many old playfellows of the Devil spring up suddenly from their beds, and strike at him treacherously; while he, without a cuff, laughed and made grimaces in the 20 corner of the room.

Essex. Instantly on hearing of thy arrival from Ireland, I sent a message to thee, good Edmund, that I might learn, from one so judicious and dispassionate as thou art, the real state of things in
5 that distracted country; it having pleased the Queen's Majesty to think of appointing me her deputy, in order to bring the rebellious to submission.

Spenser. Wisely and well considered; but more
10 worthily of her judgment than her affection. May your lordship overcome, as you have ever done, the difficulties and dangers you foresee.

Essex. We grow weak by striking at random; and knowing that I must strike, and strike heavily, I
15 would fain see exactly where the stroke shall fall.

.   .   .   .   .

Now what tale have you for us?

Spenser. Interrogate me, my lord, that I may answer each question distinctly, my mind being in sad confusion at what I have seen and undergone.
20   *Essex.* Give me thy account and opinion of these very affairs as thou leftest them; for I would rather know one part well than all imperfectly; and the violences of which I have heard within the day surpass belief.

Why weepest thou, my gentle Spenser?   Have the
rebels sacked thy house?

Spenser. They have plundered and utterly destroyed it.

Essex. I grieve for thee, and will see thee 5
righted.

Spenser. In this they have little harmed me.

Essex. How! I have heard it reported that thy
grounds are fertile, and thy mansion large and
pleasant.   10

Spenser. If river and lake and meadow-ground and
mountain could render any place the abode of pleas-
antness, pleasant was mine, indeed!

On the lovely banks of Mulla I found deep con-
tentment.   Under the dark alders did I muse and 15
meditate.   Innocent hopes were my gravest cares,
and my playfullest fancy was with kindly wishes.
Ah! surely of all cruelties the worst is to extinguish
our kindness.   Mine is gone: I love the people and
the land no longer.   My lord, ask me not about 20
them: I may speak injuriously.

Essex. Think rather, then, of thy happier hours
and busier occupations; these likewise may instruct
me.

Spenser. The first seeds I sowed in the garden, 25
ere the old castle was made habitable for my lovely
bride, were acorns from Penshurst.   I planted a
little oak before my mansion at the birth of each
child.   My sons, I said to myself, shall often play
in the shade of them when I am gone; and every 30
year shall they take the measure of their growth, as
fondly as I take theirs.

Essex. Well, well; but let not this thought make thee weep so bitterly.

Spenser. Poison may ooze from beautiful plants; deadly grief from dearest reminiscences.

5 I *must* grieve, I *must* weep: it seems the law of God, and the only one that men are not disposed to contravene. In the performance of this alone do they effectually aid one another.

Essex. Spenser! I wish I had at hand any argu-
10 ments or persuasions of force sufficient to remove thy sorrow; but, really, I am not in the habit of see-ing men grieve at anything except the loss of favour at court, or of a hawk, or of a buck-hound. And were I to swear out my condolences to a man of thy
15 discernment, in the same round roll-call phrases we employ with one another upon these occasions, I should be guilty, not of insincerity, but of insolence. True grief hath ever something sacred in it; and, when it visiteth a wise man and a brave one, is most
20 holy.

Nay, kiss not my hand: he whom God smiteth hath God with him. In his presence what am I?

Spenser. Never so great, my lord, as at this hour, when you see aright who is greater. May he guide
25 your counsels, and preserve your life and glory!

Essex. Where are thy friends? Are they with thee?

Spenser. Ah, where, indeed! Generous, true-hearted Philip! where art thou, whose presence was
30 unto me peace and safety; whose smile was con-tentment, and whose praise renown? My lord! I cannot but think of him among still heavier losses:

he was my earliest friend, and would have taught me wisdom.

Essex. Pastoral poetry, my dear Spenser, doth not require tears and lamentations. Dry thine eyes; rebuild thine house: the Queen and Council, I ven- 5 ture to promise thee, will make ample amends for every evil thou hast sustained. What! does that enforce thee to wail yet louder?

Spenser. Pardon me, bear with me, most noble heart! I have lost what no Council, no Queen, no 10 Essex, can restore.

Essex. We will see that. There are other swords, and other arms to wield them, beside a Leicester's and a Raleigh's. Others can crush their enemies, and serve their friends.   15

Spenser. O my sweet child! And of many so powerful, many so wise and so beneficent, was there none to save thee? None! none!

Essex. I now perceive that thou lamentest what almost every father is destined to lament. Happi- 20 ness must be bought, although the payment may be delayed. Consider; the same calamity might have befallen thee here in London. Neither the houses of ambassadors, nor the palaces of kings, nor the altars of God himself, are asylums against death. 25 How do I know but under this very roof there may sleep some latent calamity, that in an instant shall cover with gloom every inmate of the house, and every far dependent?

Spenser. God avert it!   30

Essex. Every day, every hour of the year, do hundreds mourn what thou mournest.

Spenser. Oh, no, no, no! Calamities there are around us; calamities there are all over the earth; calamities there are in all seasons: but none in any season, none in any place, like mine.

5 *Essex.* So say all fathers, so say all husbands. Look at any old mansion-house, and let the sun shine as gloriously as it may on the golden vanes, or the arms recently quartered over the gateway or the embayed window, and on the happy pair that haply 10 is toying at it: nevertheless, thou mayest say that of a certainty the same fabric hath seen much sorrow within its chambers, and heard many wailings; and each time this was the heaviest stroke of all. Funerals have passed along through the stout-15 hearted knights upon the wainscot, and amid the laughing nymphs upon the arras. Old servants have shaken their heads, as if somebody had deceived them, when they found that beauty and nobility could perish.

20 Edmund! the things that are too true pass by us as if they were not true at all; and when they have singled us out, then only do they strike us. Thou and I must go too. Perhaps the next year may blow us away with its fallen leaves.*

25 *Spenser.* For you, my lord, many years (I trust) are waiting: I never shall see those fallen leaves. No leaf, no bud, will spring upon the earth before I sink into her breast for ever.

Essex. Thou, who art wiser than most men, 30 shouldst bear with patience, equanimity, and courage what is common to all.

Spenser. Enough, enough, enough! Have all men

* It happened so.

seen their infant burned to ashes before their eyes?

Essex. Gracious God! Merciful Father! what is this?

Spenser. Burned alive! burned to ashes! burned 5
to ashes! The flames dart their serpent tongues
through the nursery-window. I cannot quit thee,
my Elizabeth! I cannot lay down our Edmund!
Oh, these flames! They persecute, they enthrall
me; they curl round my temples; they hiss upon 10
my brain; they taunt me with their fierce, foul
voices; they carp at me, they wither me, they con-
sume me, throwing back to me a little of life to roll
and suffer in, with their fangs upon me. Ask me,
my lord, the things you wish to know from me: I 15
may answer them; I am now composed again.
Command me, my gracious lord! I would yet
serve you: soon I shall be unable. You have
stooped to raise me up; you have borne with me;
you have pitied me, even like one not powerful. 20
You have brought comfort, and will leave it with me;
for gratitude is comfort.

Oh! my memory stands all a tip-toe on one burning point: when it drops from it, then it perishes.
Spare me; ask me nothing; let me weep before you 25
in peace,—the kindest act of greatness.

Essex. I should rather have dared to mount into
the midst of the conflagration than I now dare
entreat thee not to weep. The tears that overflow
thy heart, my Spenser, will staunch and heal it in 30
their sacred stream; but not without hope in God.

Spenser. My hope in God is that I may soon see

again what he has taken from me. Amid the myriads of angels, there is not one so beautiful; and even he (if there be any) who is appointed my guardian could never love me so. Ah! these are idle 5 thoughts, vain wanderings, distempered dreams. If there ever were guardian angels, he who so wanted one—my helpless boy—would not have left these arms upon my knees.

Essex. God help and sustain thee, too gentle 10 Spenser! I never will desert thee. But what am I? Great they have called me! Alas, how powerless then and infantile is greatness in the presence of calamity!

Come, give me thy hand: let us walk up and 15 down the gallery. Bravely done! I will envy no more a Sidney or a Raleigh.

The Lady Lisle and Elizabeth Gaunt.

Lady Lisle. Madam, I am confident you will pardon me; for affliction teaches forgiveness.

Elizabeth Gaunt. From the cell of the condemned we are going, unless my hopes mislead me, where alone we can receive it.　　　　　　　　　　5

Tell me, I beseech you, lady! in what matter or manner do you think you can have offended a poor sinner such as I am. Surely we come into this dismal place for our offences; and it is not here that any can be given or taken.　　　　　　　　　10

Lady Lisle. Just now, when I entered the prison, I saw your countenance serene and cheerful; you looked upon me for a time with an unaltered eye; you turned away from me, as I fancied, only to utter some expressions of devotion; and again you looked 15 upon me, and tears rolled down your face. Alas that I should, by any circumstance, any action or recollection, make another unhappy! Alas that I should deepen the gloom in the very shadow of death!　　　　　　　　　　　　　　20

Elizabeth Gaunt. Be comforted: you have not done it. Grief softens and melts and flows away with tears.

I wept because another was greatly more wretched than myself. I wept at that black attire—at that 25 attire of modesty and of widowhood.

Lady Lisle. It covers a wounded, almost a broken heart—an unworthy offering to our blessed Redeemer.

Elizabeth Gaunt. In his name let us now rejoice! 5 Let us offer our prayers and our thanks at once together! We may yield up our souls, perhaps, at the same hour.

Lady Lisle. Is mine so pure? Have I bemoaned, as I should have done, the faults I have committed? 10 Have my sighs arisen for the unmerited mercies of my God; and not rather for him, the beloved of my heart, the adviser and sustainer I have lost?

Open, O gates of Death!

Smile on me, approve my last action in this world, 15 O virtuous husband! O saint and martyr! my brave, compassionate, and loving Lisle!

Elizabeth Gaunt. And cannot you, too, smile, sweet lady? Are not you with him even now? Doth body, doth clay, doth air, separate and estrange free 20 spirits? Bethink you of his gladness, of his glory; and begin to partake them.

Oh! how could an Englishman, how could twelve, condemn to death—condemn to so great an evil as they thought it and may find it—this innocent and 25 helpless widow?

Lady Lisle. Blame not *that* jury!—blame not the jury which brought against me the verdict of guilty. I was so: I received in my house a wanderer who had fought under the rash and giddy Monmouth. 30 He was hungry and thirsty, and I took him in. My Saviour had commanded, my King had forbidden it.

Yet the twelve would not have delivered me over

to death, unless the judge had threatened them
with an accusation of treason in default of it.
Terror made them unanimous: they redeemed their
properties and lives at the stated price.

Elizabeth Gaunt. I hope, at least, the unfortunate 5
man whom you received in the hour of danger may
avoid his penalty.

Lady Lisle. Let us hope it.

Elizabeth Gaunt. I, too, am imprisoned for the
same offence; and I have little expectation that he 10
who was concealed by me hath any chance of happiness, although he hath escaped. Could I find the
means of conveying to him a small pittance, I should
leave the world the more comfortably.

Lady Lisle. Trust in God; not in one thing or 15
another, but in all. Resign the care of this wanderer
to *his* guidance.

Elizabeth Gaunt. He abandoned that guidance.

Lady Lisle. Unfortunate! how can money then
avail him? 20

Elizabeth Gaunt. It might save him from distress
and from despair, from the taunts of the hard-
hearted, and from the inclemency of the godly.

Lady Lisle. In godliness, O my friend! there cannot be inclemency. 25

Elizabeth Gaunt. You are thinking of perfection,
my dear lady; and I marvel not at it, for what else
hath ever occupied your thoughts! But godliness,
in almost the best of us, often is austere, often
uncompliant and rigid—proner to reprove than to 30
pardon, to drag back or thrust aside than to invite
and help onward.

Poor man! I never knew him before; I cannot tell how he shall endure his self-reproach, or whether it will bring him to calmer thoughts hereafter.

Lady Lisle. I am not a busy idler in curiosity; nor, if I were, is there time enough left me for indulging in it; yet gladly would I learn the history of events, at the first appearance so resembling those in mine.

Elizabeth Gaunt. The person's name I never may disclose; which would be the worst thing I could betray of the trust he placed in me. He took refuge in my humble dwelling, imploring me in the name of Christ to harbour him for a season. Food and raiment were afforded him unsparingly; yet his fears made him shiver through them. Whatever I could urge of prayer and exhortation was not wanting; still, although he prayed, he was disquieted. Soon came to my ears the declaration of the King, that his Majesty would rather pardon a rebel than the concealer of a rebel. The hope was a faint one; but it *was* a hope, and I gave it him. His thanksgivings were now more ardent, his prayers more humble, and oftener repeated. They did not strengthen his heart: it was unpurified and unprepared for them. Poor creature! he consented with it to betray me; and I am condemned to be burned alive. Can we believe, can we encourage the hope, that in his weary way through life he will find those only who will conceal from him the knowledge of this execution? Heavily, too heavily, must it weigh on so irresolute and infirm a breast.

Let it not move you to weeping.

Lady Lisle. It does not; oh! it does not.

Elizabeth Gaunt. What, then?

Lady Lisle. Your saintly tenderness, your heavenly tranquillity.

Elizabeth Gaunt. No, no: abstain! abstain! It was 5 I who grieved; it was I who doubted. Let us now be firmer: we have both the same rock to rest upon. See! I shed no tears.

I saved his life, an unprofitable and (I fear) a joy-less one; he, by God's grace, has thrown open to 10 me, and at an earlier hour than ever I ventured to expect it, the avenue to eternal bliss.

Lady Lisle. O my good angel! that bestrewest with fresh flowers a path already smooth and pleas-ant to me, may those timorous men who have 15 betrayed, and those misguided ones who have prose-cuted us, be conscious on their death-beds that we have entered it! and they too will at last find rest.

Tbe Empress Catbarine and Princess Dasbkof.

Catharine. Into his heart! into his heart! If he escapes, we perish.

Do you think, Dashkof, they can hear me through the double door? Yes; hark! they heard me: they
5 have done it.

What bubbling and gurgling! he groaned but once.

Listen! his blood is busier now than it ever was before. I should not have thought it could have
10 splashed so loud upon the floor, although our bed, indeed, is rather of the highest.

Put your ear against the lock.

Dashkof. I hear nothing.

Catharine. My ears are quicker than yours, and
15 know these notes better. Let me come.—Hear nothing! You did not wait long enough, nor with coolness and patience. There!—there again! The drops are now like lead: every half-minute they penetrate the eider-down and the mattress.—How
20 now! which of these fools has brought his dog with him? What tramping and lapping! the creature will carry the marks all about the palace with his feet and muzzle.

Dashkof. Oh, heavens!

25 *Catharine.* Are you afraid?

Dashkof. There is a horror that surpasses fear, and will have none of it. I knew not this before.

Catharine. You turn pale and tremble. You should have supported me, in case I had required it.

Dashkof. I thought only of the tyrant. Neither 5 in life nor in death could any one of these miscreants make me tremble. But the husband slain by his wife!—I saw not into my heart; I looked not into it, and it chastises me.

Catharine. Dashkof, are you, then, really unwell? 10

Dashkof. What will Russia, what will Europe, say?

Catharine. Russia has no more voice than a whale. She may toss about in her turbulence; but my artillery (for now, indeed, I can safely call it 15 mine) shall stun and quiet her.

Dashkof. God grant——

Catharine. I cannot but laugh at thee, my pretty Dashkof! God grant, forsooth! He has granted all we wanted from him at present—the safe re- 20 moval of this odious Peter.

Dashkof. Yet Peter loved *you ;* and even the worst husband must leave, surely, the recollection of some sweet moments. The sternest must have trembled, both with apprehension and with hope, 25 at the first alteration in the health of his consort; at the first promise of true union, imperfect without progeny. Then, there are thanks rendered together to heaven, and satisfactions communicated, and infant words interpreted; and when the one 30 has failed to pacify the sharp cries of babyhood, pettish and impatient as sovereignty itself, the success of the other in calming it, and the unenvied triumph of this exquisite ambition, and the calm gazes that it wins upon it.

Catharine. Are these, my sweet friend, your
5 lessons from the Stoic school? Are not they, rather, the pale-faced reflections of some kind epithalamiast from Livonia or Bessarabia? Come, come away. I am to know nothing at present of the deplorable occurrence. Did not you wish his death?
10 *Dashkof.* It is not his death that shocks me.

Catharine. I understand you: beside, you said as much before.

Dashkof. I fear for your renown.

Catharine. And for your own good name—ay,
15 Dashkof?

Dashkof. He was not, nor did I ever wish him to be, my friend.

Catharine. You hated him.

Dashkof. Even hatred may be plucked up too
20 roughly.

Catharine. Europe shall be informed of my rea-sons, if she should ever find out that I counte-nanced the conspiracy. She shall be persuaded that her repose made the step necessary; that my
25 own life was in danger; that I fell upon my knees to soften the conspirators; that, only when I had fainted, the horrible deed was done. She knows already that Peter was always ordering new exer-cises and uniforms; and my ministers can evince
30 at the first audience my womanly love of peace.

Dashkof. Europe may be more easily subjugated than duped.

Catharine. She shall be both, God willing.

Dashkof. The majesty of thrones will seem endangered by this open violence.

Catharine. The majesty of thrones is never in jeopardy by those who sit upon them. A sovereign 5 may cover one with blood more safely than a subject can pluck a feather out of the cushion. It is only when the people does the violence that we hear an ill report of it. Kings poison and stab one another in pure legitimacy. Do your republican 10 ideas revolt from such a doctrine?

Dashkof. I do not question this right of theirs, and never will oppose their exercise of it. But if you prove to the people how easy a matter it is to extinguish an emperor, and how pleasantly and 15 prosperously we may live after it, is it not probable that they also will now and then try the experiment; particularly, if any one in Russia should hereafter hear of glory and honour, and how immortal are these by the consent of mankind, in all countries 20 and ages, in him who releases the world, or any part of it, from a lawless and ungovernable despot? The chances of escape are many, and the greater if he should have no accomplices. Of his renown there is no doubt at all: that is placed above 25 chance and beyond time, by the sword he hath exercised so righteously.

Catharine. True; but we must reason like democrats no longer. Republicanism is the best thing we can have, when we cannot have power; but no 30 one ever held the two together. I am now autocrat.

Dashkof. Truly, then, may I congratulate you. The dignity is the highest a mortal can attain.

Catharine. I know and feel it.

Dashkof. I wish you always may.

5 *Catharine.* I doubt not the stability of power: I can make constant both fortune and love. My Dashkof smiles at this conceit: she has here the same advantage, and does not envy her friend even the autocracy.

10 *Dashkof.* Indeed I do, and most heartily.

Catharine. How?

Dashkof. I know very well what those intended who first composed the word; but they blundered egregiously. In spite of them, it signifies power 15 over oneself—of all power the most enviable, and the least consistent with power over others.

I hope and trust there is no danger to you from any member of the council-board inflaming the guards or other soldiery.

20 *Catharine.* The members of the council-board did not sit *at* it, but *upon* it; and their tactics were performed cross-legged. What partisans are to be dreaded of that commander-in-chief whose chief command is over pantaloons and facings, whose ut- 25 most glory is perched on loops and feathers, and who fancies that battles are to be won rather by pointing the hat than the cannon?

Dashkof. Peter was not insensible to glory; few men are: but wiser heads than his have been per- 30 plexed in the road to it, and many have lost it by their ardour to attain it. I have always said that, unless we devote ourselves to the public good, we may perhaps be celebrated; but it is beyond the power of fortune, or even of genius, to exalt us above the dust.

Catharine. Dashkof, you are a sensible, sweet creature; but rather too romantic on *principle*, and 5 rather too visionary on glory. I shall always both esteem and love you; but no other woman in Europe will be great enough to endure you, and you will really put the men *hors de combat.* Thinking is an enemy to beauty, and no friend to tenderness. Men 10 can ill brook it one in another; in women it renders them what they would fain call "scornful" (vain assumption of high prerogative!) and what you would find bestial and outrageous. As for my reputation, which I know is dear to you, I can pur-15 chase all the best writers in Europe with a snuff-box each, and all the remainder with its contents. Not a gentleman of the Academy but is enchanted by a toothpick, if I deign to send it him. A brilliant makes me Semiramis; a watch-chain, 20 Venus; a ring, Juno. Voltaire is my friend.

Dashkof. He was Frederick's.

Catharine. I shall be the *Pucelle* of Russia. No! I had forgotten; he has treated her scandalously.

Dashkof. Does your Majesty value the flatteries 25 of a writer who ridicules the most virtuous and glorious of his nation; who crouched before that monster of infamy, Louis XV.; and that worse monster, the king his predecessor? He reviled, with every indignity and indecency, the woman 30 who rescued France; and who alone, of all that ever led the armies of that kingdom, made its

conquerors—the English—tremble. Its monarchs
and marshals cried and ran like capons, flapping
their fine crests from wall to wall, and cackling at
one breath defiance and surrender. The village
5 girl drew them back into battle, and placed the
heavens themselves against the enemies of Charles.
She seemed supernatural: the English recruits
deserted; they would not fight against God.

Catharine. Fools and bigots!

10 *Dashkof.* The whole world contained none other,
excepting those who fed upon them. The Maid of
Orleans was pious and sincere: her life asserted it;
her death confirmed it. Glory to her, Catharine, if
you love glory. Detestation to him who has pro-
15 faned the memory of this most holy martyr—the
guide and avenger of her king, the redeemer and
saviour of her country.

Catharine. Be it so; but Voltaire buoys me up
above some impertinent, troublesome qualms.

20 *Dashkof.* If Deism had been prevalent in Europe,
he would have been the champion of Christianity;
and if the French had been Protestants, he would
have shed tears upon the papal slipper. He buoys up
no one: for he gives no one hope. He may amuse:
25 dulness itself must be amused, indeed, by the
versatility and brilliancy of his wit.

Catharine. While I was meditating on the great
action I have now so happily accomplished, I sometimes thought his wit feeble. This idea, no doubt,
30 originated from the littleness of everything in
comparison with my undertaking.

Dashkof. Alas! we lose much when we lose the

capacity of being delighted by men of genius, and gain little when we are forced to run to them for incredulity.

Catharine. I shall make some use of my philosopher at Ferney. I detest him as much as you do; but where will you find me another who writes so pointedly? You really, then, fancy that people care for truth? Innocent Dashkof! Believe me, there is nothing so delightful in life as to find a liar in a person of repute. Have you never heard good folks rejoicing at it? Or, rather, can you mention to me any one who has not been in raptures when he could communicate such glad tidings? The goutiest man would go on foot without a crutch to tell his friend of it at midnight; and would cross the Neva for the purpose, when he doubted whether the ice would bear him. Men, in general, are so weak in truth, that they are obliged to put their bravery under it to prop it. Why do they pride themselves, think you, on their courage, when the bravest of them is by many degrees less courageous than a mastiff-bitch in the straw? It is only that they may be rogues without hearing it, and make their fortunes without rendering an account of them.

Now we chat again as we used to do. Your spirits and your enthusiasm have returned. Courage, my sweet Dashkof; do not begin to sigh again. We never can want husbands while we are young and lively. Alas! I cannot always be so. Heigho! But serfs and preferment will do: none shall refuse me at ninety—Paphos or Tobolsk.

Have not you a song for me?

Dashkof. German or Russian?

Catharine. Neither, neither. Some frightful word might drop—might remind me—no, nothing
5 shall remind me. French, rather: French songs are the liveliest in the world.

Is the rouge off my face?

Dashkof. It is rather in streaks and mottles; excepting just under the eyes, where it sits as it
10 should do.

Catharine. I am heated and thirsty: I cannot imagine how. I think we have not yet taken our coffee—was it so strong? What am I dreaming of? I could eat only a slice of melon at breakfast; my duty
15 urged me *then*, and dinner is yet to come. Remember, I am to faint at the midst of it when the intelligence comes in, or rather when, in despite of every effort to conceal it from me, the awful truth has flashed upon my mind. Remember, too, you are to
20 catch me, and to cry for help, and to tear those fine flaxen hairs which we laid up together on the toilet; and we are both to be as inconsolable as we can be for the life of us. Not now, child, not now. Come, sing. I know not how to fill up the interval.
25 Two long hours yet!—how stupid and tiresome! I wish all things of the sort could be done and be over in a day. They are mightily disagreeable when by nature one is not cruel. People little know my character. I have the tenderest heart upon earth.
30 I am courageous, but I am full of weaknesses. I possess in perfection the higher part of men, and— to a friend I may say it—the most amiable part of

women. Ho, ho! at last you smile: now your
thoughts upon that.

Dashkof. I have heard fifty men swear it.

Catharine. They lied, the knaves! I hardly knew
them by sight. We were talking of the sad ne- 5
cessity.—Ivan must follow next: he is heir to the
throne. I have a wild, impetuous, pleasant little
protégé, who shall attempt to rescue him. I will
have him persuaded and incited to it, and assured
of pardon on the scaffold. He can never know the 10
trick we play him; unless his head, like a bottle of
Bordeaux, ripens its contents in the sawdust. Orders are given that Ivan be despatched at the first
disturbance in the precincts of the castle; in short,
at the fire of the sentry. But not now,—another 15
time: two such scenes together, and without some
interlude, would perplex people.

I thought we spoke of singing: do not make me
wait, my dearest creature! Now cannot you sing
as usual, without smoothing your dove's-throat with 20
your handkerchief, and taking off your necklace?
Give it me, then; give it me. I will hold it for
you: I must play with something.

Sing, sing; I am quite impatient.

Leofric and Godiva.

Godiva. There is a dearth in the land, my sweet
Leofric! Remember how many weeks of drought we
have had, even in the deep pastures of Leicester-
shire; and how many Sundays we have heard the
5 same prayers for rain, and supplications that it would
please the Lord in his mercy to turn aside his anger
from the poor, pining cattle. You, my dear husband, have imprisoned more than one malefactor
for leaving his dead ox in the public way; and other
10 hinds have fled before you out of the traces, in
which they, and their sons and their daughters, and
haply their old fathers and mothers, were dragging
the abandoned wain homeward. Although we were
accompanied by many brave spearmen and skilful
15 archers, it was perilous to pass the creatures which
the farm-yard dogs, driven from the hearth by the
poverty of their masters, were tearing and devour-
ing; while others, bitten and lamed, filled the air
either with long and deep howls or sharp and quick
20 barkings, as they struggled with hunger and feebleness, or were exasperated by heat and pain. Nor
could the thyme from the heath, nor the bruised
branches of the fir-tree, extinguish or abate the foul
odour.
25 *Leofric.* And now, Godiva, my darling, thou art
afraid we should be eaten up before we enter the

111

gates of Coventry; or perchance that in the gardens
there are no roses to greet thee, no sweet herbs for
thy mat and pillow.

Godiva. Leofric, I have no such fears. This is
the month of roses: I find them everywhere since 5
my blessed marriage. They, and all other sweet
herbs, I know not why, seem to greet me wherever
I look at them, as though they knew and expected
me. Surely they cannot feel that I am fond of
them. 10

Leofric. O light, laughing simpleton! But what
wouldst thou? I came not hither to pray; and yet
if praying would satisfy thee, or remove the drought,
I would ride up straightway to Saint Michael's and
pray until morning. 15

Godiva. I would do the same, O Leofric! but God
hath turned away his ear from holier lips than mine.
Would my own dear husband hear me, if I implored
him for what is easier to accomplish,—what he can
do like God? 20

Leofric. How! what is it?

Godiva. I would not, in the first hurry of your
wrath, appeal to you, my loving Lord, in behalf of
these unhappy men who have offended you.

Leofric. Unhappy! is that all? 25

Godiva. Unhappy they must surely be, to have
offended you so grievously. What a soft air breathes
over us! how quiet and serene and still an evening!
how calm are the heavens and the earth!—Shall none
enjoy them; not even we, my Leofric? The sun is 30
ready to set: let it never set, O Leofric, on your
anger. These are not my words: they are better

than mine. Should they lose their virtue from my unworthiness in uttering them?

Leofric. Godiva, wouldst thou plead to me for rebels?

5 *Godiva.* They have, then, drawn the sword against you? Indeed, I knew it not.

Leofric. They have omitted to send me my dues, established by my ancestors, well knowing of our nuptials, and of the charges and festivities they re-
10 quire, and that in a season of such scarcity my own lands are insufficient.

Godiva. If they were starving, as they said they were——

Leofric. Must I starve too? Is it not enough to
15 lose my vassals?

Godiva. Enough! O God! too much! too much! May you never lose them! Give them life, peace, comfort, contentment. There are those among them who kissed me in my infancy, and who blessed
20 me at the baptismal font. Leofric, Leofric! the first old man I meet I shall think is one of those; and I shall think on the blessing he gave, and (ah me!) on the blessing I bring back to him. My heart will bleed, will burst; and he will weep at it! he will
25 weep, poor soul, for the wife of a cruel lord who denounces vengeance on him, who carries death into his family!

Leofric. We must hold solemn festivals.

Godiva. We must, indeed.

30 *Leofric.* Well, then?

Godiva. Is the clamorousness that succeeds the death of God's dumb creatures, are crowded halls,

are slaughtered cattle, festivals?—are maddening
songs, and giddy dances, and hireling praises from
parti-coloured coats? Can the voice of a minstrel
tell us better things of ourselves than our own in-
ternal one might tell us; or can his breath make our 5
breath softer in sleep? O my beloved! let everything be a joyance to us: it will, if we will. Sad is
the day, and worse must follow, when we hear
the blackbird in the garden, and do not throb with
joy. But, Leofric, the high festival is strown by 10
the servant of God upon the heart of man. It is
gladness, it is thanksgiving; it is the orphan, the
starveling, pressed to the bosom, and bidden as its
first commandment to remember its benefactor.
We will hold this festival; the guests are ready: we 15
may keep it up for weeks, and months, and years
together, and always be the happier and the richer
for it. The beverage of this feast, O Leofric, is
sweeter than bee or flower or vine can give us: it
flows from heaven; and in heaven will it abundantly 20
be poured out again to him who pours it out here
unsparingly.

Leofric. Thou art wild.

Godiva. I have, indeed, lost myself. Some Power,
some good kind Power, melts me (body and soul 25
and voice) into tenderness and love. O my husband, we must obey it. Look upon me! look upon
me! lift your sweet eyes from the ground! I will
not cease to supplicate; I dare not.

Leofric. We may think upon it.   30

Godiva. Never say that! What! think upon
goodness when you can be good? Let not the

infants cry for sustenance! The mother of our blessed Lord will hear them; us never, never afterward.

Leofric. Here comes the Bishop: we are but one 5 mile from the walls. Why dismountest thou? no bishop can expect it. Godiva! my honour and rank among men are humbled by this. Earl Godwin will hear of it. Up! up! the Bishop hath seen it: he urgeth his horse onward. Dost thou not hear him 10 now upon the solid turf behind thee?

Godiva. Never, no, never will I rise, O Leofric, until you remit this most impious tax,—this tax on hard labour, on hard life.

Leofric. Turn round: look how the fat nag canters, 15 as to the tune of a sinner's psalm, slow and hard-breathing. What reason or right can the people have to complain, while their bishop's steed is so sleek and well caparisoned? Inclination to change, desire to abolish old usages.—Up! up! for shame! 20 They shall smart for it, idlers! Sir Bishop, I must blush for my young bride.

Godiva. My husband, my husband! will you pardon the city?

Leofric. Sir Bishop! I could not think you would 25 have seen her in this plight. Will I pardon? Yea, Godiva, by the holy rood, will I pardon the city, when thou ridest naked at noontide through the streets!

Godiva. O my dear, cruel Leofric, where is the 30 heart you gave me? It was not so: can mine have hardened it?

Bishop. Earl, thou abashest thy spouse; she

turneth pale, and weepeth. Lady Godiva, peace be
with thee.

Godiva. Thanks, holy man! peace will be with me
when peace is with your city.   Did you hear my
Lord's cruel word?   5

Bishop. I did, lady.

Godiva. Will you remember it, and pray against it.

Bishop. Wilt *thou* forget it, daughter?

Godiva. I am not offended.

Bishop. Angel of peace and purity   10

Godiva. But treasure it up in your heart: deem it
an incense, good only when it is consumed and
spent, ascending with prayer and sacrifice.   And,
now, what was it?

Bishop. Christ save us! that he will pardon the city 15
when thou ridest naked through the streets at noon.

Godiva. Did he not swear an oath?

Bishop. He sware by the holy rood.

Godiva. My Redeemer, thou hast heard it! save
the city!   20

Leofric. We are now upon the beginning of the
pavement: these are the suburbs.   Let us think of
feasting: we may pray afterward; to-morrow we
shall rest.

Godiva. No judgments, then, to-morrow, Leofric? 25

Leofric. None: we will carouse.

Godiva. The saints of heaven have given me
strength and confidence; my prayers are heard; the
heart of my beloved is now softened.

Leofric (aside). Ay, ay—they shall smart, though. 30

Godiva. Say, dearest Leofric, is there indeed no
other hope, no other mediation?

Leofric. I have sworn. Beside, thou hast made me redden and turn my face away from thee, and all the knaves have seen it: this adds to the city's crime.

5 *Godiva.* I have blushed too, Leofric, and was not rash nor obdurate.

Leofric. But thou, my sweetest, art given to blushing: there is no conquering it in thee. I wish thou hadst not alighted so hastily and roughly: it 10 hath shaken down a sheaf of thy hair. Take heed thou sit not upon it, lest it anguish thee. Well done! it mingleth now sweetly with the cloth of gold upon the saddle, running here and there, as if it had life and faculties and business, and were 15 working thereupon some newer and cunninger device. O my beauteous Eve! there is a Paradise about thee! the world is refreshed as thou movest and breathest on it. I cannot see or think of evil where thou art. I could throw my arms even here 20 about thee. No signs for me! no shaking of sun-beams! no reproof or frown or wonderment—I *will* say it—now then for worse—I could close with my kisses thy half-open lips, ay, and those lovely and loving eyes, before the people.

25 *Godiva.* To-morrow you shall kiss me, and they shall bless you for it. I shall be very pale, for to-night I must fast and pray.

Leofric. I do not hear thee; the voices of the folk are so loud under this archway.

30 *Godiva (to herself).* God help them! good kind souls! I hope they will not crowd about me so to-morrow. O Leofric! could my name be forgotten,

and yours alone remembered! But perhaps my
innocence may save me from reproach; and how
many as innocent are in fear and famine! No eye
will open on me but fresh from tears. What a
young mother for so large a family! Shall my 5
youth harm me? Under God's hand it gives me
courage. Ah! when will the morning come? Ah!
when will the noon be over?

The story of Godiva, at one of whose festivals or fairs I was
present in my boyhood, has always much interested me ; and I 10
wrote a poem on it, sitting, I remember, by the *square pool* at
Rugby. When I showed it to the friend in whom I had most
confidence, he began to scoff at the subject ; and, on his reaching
the last line, his laughter was loud and immoderate. This Conversation has brought both laughter and stanza back to me, and 15
the earnestness with which I entreated and implored my friend
not to tell the lads, so heart-strickenly and desperately was
I ashamed. The verses are these, if any one else should wish
another laugh at me :

In every hour, in every mood,   20
O lady, it is sweet and good
  To bathe the soul in prayer;
And, at the close of such a day,
When we have ceased to bless and pray,
  To dream on thy long hair.   25

May the peppermint be still growing on the bank in that place !

W. S. L.

Vittoria Colonna
and Michel-Angelo Buonarrotti.

* * * * * * *

Vittoria. It was beautifully and piously said in
days of old, that, wherever a spring rises from the
earth, an altar should be erected. Ought not we,
my friend, to bear the same veneration to the genius
5 which springs from obscurity in the loneliness of
lofty places, and which descends to irrigate the
pastures of the mind with a perennial freshness and
vivifying force? If great poets build their own
temples, as indeed they do, let us at least offer up
10 to them our praises and thanksgivings, and hope to
render them acceptable by the purest incense of the
heart.

Michel-Angelo. First, we must find the priests;
for ours are inconvertible from* their crumbling
15 altars. Too surely we are without an Aristoteles
to precede and direct them.

Vittoria. We want him, not only for poetry, but
philosophy. Much of the dusty perfumery, which
thickened for a season the pure air of Attica, was
20 dissipated by his breath. Calm reasoning, deep
investigation, patient experiment, succeeded to con-
tentious quibbles and trivial irony. The sun of
Aristoteles dispersed the unwholesome vapour that
arose from the garden of Academus. Instead of

spectral demons, instead of the monstrous progeny
of mystery and immodesty, there arose tangible
images of perfect symmetry.   Homer was recalled
from banishment; Æschylus followed; the choruses
bowed before him, divided, and took their stands. 5
Symphonies were heard,—what symphonies! so
powerful as to lighten the chain that Jupiter had
riveted on his rival.   The conquerors of kings until
then omnipotent,—kings who had trampled on the
towers of Babylon, and had shaken the eternal 10
sanctuaries of Thebes,—the conquerors of these
kings bowed their olive-crowned heads to the
sceptre of Destiny, and their tears ran profusely
over the immeasurable wilderness of human woes.

Michel-Angelo. We have no poetry of this kind 15
now, nor have we auditors who could estimate or
know it if we had.   Yet, as the fine arts have raised
up their own judges, literature may, ere long, do the
same.   Instead of undervaluing and beating down,
let us acknowledge and praise any resemblance we 20.
may trace to the lineaments of a past and stronger
generation.

Vittoria. But, by the manners and habitudes
of antiquity, ours are little to be improved.
Scholars who scorn the levity of Ariosto, and 25
speak disdainfully of the Middle Ages, in the very
centre of the enchantment thrown over them by the
magician of Ferrara, never think how much we owe,
not only to him, but also to those ages: never think
by what energies, corporeal and mental, from the bar- 30
barous soldier rose the partially polished knight;
and high above him, by slower degrees, the accom-

plished and perfect gentleman, the summit of nobility.

Michel-Angelo. Oh that Pescara were present!— Pescara! whom your words seem to have embodied 5 and recalled!—Pescara! the lover of all glory, but mostly of yours, Madonna!—he to whom your beauty was eloquence and your eloquence beauty, inseparable as the influences of Deity.

Vittoria. Present! and is he not? Where I am, 10 there is he, for evermore. Earth may divide; Heaven never does. The beauty you speak of is the only thing departed from me, and that also is with him, perhaps. He may—I hope he may—see me as he left me; only more pacified, more resigned. 15 After I had known Pescara, even if I had never been his, I should have been espoused to him; espoused to him before the assembled testimonies of his innumerable virtues,—before his genius, his fortitude, his respectful superiority, his manly 20 gentleness. Yes, I should have been married to his glory; and, neither in his lifetime nor when he left the world, would I have endured, O Michel-Angelo, any other alliance. The very thought, the very words conveying it, are impiety. But friendship 25 helps to support that heavy pall to which the devoted cling tenaciously for ever.

Michel-Angelo. Oh! that at this moment——

Vittoria. Hush! hush! Wishes are by-paths on the declivity to unhappiness: the weaker terminate 30 in the sterile sand; the stronger, the vale of tears. If there are griefs—which we know there are—so intense as to deprive us of our intellects, griefs in

the next degree of intensity, far from depriving us
of them, amplify, purify, regulate, and adorn them.
We sometimes spring above happiness, and fall on
the other side. This hath happened to me; but
strength enough is left me to raise myself up again, 5
and to follow the guide who calls me.

Michel-Angelo. Surely God hath shown that mortal what his own love is, for whom he hath har-
monised a responsive bosom, warm in the last as in
the first embraces. One look of sympathy, one 10
regret at parting, is enough, is too much: it bur-
dens the heart with overpayment. You cannot
gather up the blossoms which, by blast after blast,
have been scattered and whirled behind you. Are
they requisite? The fruit was formed within them 15
ere they fell upon the walk; you have culled it in its
season.

Vittoria. Before we go into another state of existence, a thousand things occur to detach us imper-
ceptibly from this. To some (who knows to how 20
many?) the images of early love return with an
inviting yet a saddening glance, and the breast that
was laid out for the sepulchre bleeds afresh. Such
are ready to follow where they are beckoned, and
look keenly into the darkness they are about to 25
penetrate.

Did we not begin to converse on another subject?
Why have you not spoken to me this half-hour?

Michel-Angelo. I see, O Donna Vittoria, I may
close the volume we were to read and criticise.   30

Vittoria. Then, I hope you have something of your
own for me instead.

Michel-Angelo. Are you not tired of my verses? Your smile is too splendid a reward, but too indistinct an answer. Pray, pray tell me, Madonna!— and yet I have hardly the courage to hear you tell
5 me—have I not sometimes written to you——

Vittoria. My cabinet can answer for that. Lift up your sphinx, if you desire to find it. Any thing in particular?

Michel-Angelo. I would say, written to you
10 with——

Vittoria. With what? A golden pen?

Michel-Angelo. No, no.

Vittoria. An adamantine one?

You child! you child! are you hiding it in my
15 sleeve? An eagle's plume? a nightingale's? a dove's? I must have recourse to the living sphinx, if there is any, not to the porphyry. Have you other pens than these? I know the traces of them all; and am unwilling to give you credit for any
20 fresh variety. But come, tell me, what is it?

Michel-Angelo. I am apprehensive that I sometimes have written to you with an irrepressible gush of tenderness, which is but narrowed and deepened and precipitated by entering the channel of verse.
25 This, falling upon vulgar ears, might be misinterpreted.

Vittoria. If I have deserved a wise man's praise and a virtuous man's affection, I am not to be defrauded of them by stealthy whispers, nor de-
30 terred from them by intemperate clamour. She whom Pescara selected for his own must excite the envy of too many; but the object of envy is not the

sufferer by it: there are those who convert it even into recreation. One star hath ruled my destiny and shaped my course. Perhaps,—no, not perhaps, but surely,—under that clear light I may enjoy unreproved the enthusiasm of his friend,—the 5 greatest man, the most ardent and universal genius, he has left behind him. Courage! courage! Lift up again the head which nothing on earth should lower. When death approaches me, be present, Michel-Angelo, and shed as pure tears on this hand 10 as I did shed on the hand of Pescara.

Michel-Angelo. Madonna, they are these; they are these! Endure them now, rather!

Merciful God! if there is piety in either, grant me to behold her at that hour, not in the palace of a 15 hero, not in the chamber of a saint, but from thine everlasting mansions!

General Kleber and French Officers.

An English officer was sitting with his back against the base of the Great Pyramid. He sometimes looked toward those of elder date and ruder materials before him, sometimes was absorbed in 5 thought, and sometimes was observed to write in a pocket-book with great rapidity.

"If he were not writing," said a French naturalist to a young ensign, "I should imagine him to have lost his eyesight by the ophthalmia. He does 10 not see us: level your rifle; we cannot find a greater curiosity."

The arts prevailed: the officer slided with extended arms from his resting-place; the blood, running from his breast, was audible as a swarm of 15 insects in the sand. No other sound was heard. Powder had exploded; life had passed away: not a vestige remained of either.

"Let us examine his papers," said the naturalist.

"Pardon me, sir," answered the ensign: "my 20 first inquiry on such occasions is *What's o'clock?* and afterward I pursue my mineralogical researches."

At these words he drew forth the dead man's watch, and stuck it into his sash, while with the 25 other hand he snatched out a purse containing some zecchins: every part of the dress was examined, and not quite fruitlessly.

"See! a locket with the miniature of a young woman!" Such it was: a modest and lovely countenance.

"Ha! ha!" said the ensign: "a few touches, a very few touches,—I can give them,—and Adela 5 will take this for me. Two inches higher, and the ball had split it: what a thoughtless man he was! There is gold in it too: it weighs heavy. Peste! an old woman at the back, gray as a cat."

It was the officer's mother, in her old age, as he 10 had left her. There was something of sweet piety, not unsaddened by presage, in the countenance. He severed it with his knife, and threw it into the bosom of her son. Two foreign letters and two pages in pencil were the contents of the pocket-15 book. Two locks of hair had fallen out: one rested on his eye-lashes, for the air was motionless, the other was drawn to the earth by his blood.

The papers were taken to General Kleber by the naturalist and his associate, with a correct recital 20 of the whole occurrence; excepting the appendages of watch, zecchins, and locket.

"Young man," said Kleber gravely, "is this a subject of merriment to you? Who knows whether you or I may not be deprived of life as suddenly 25 and unexpectedly? He was not your enemy: perhaps he was writing to a mother or sister. God help them! these suffer most from war: the heart of the far-distant is the scene of its most cruel devastations. Leave the papers; you may go: call 30 the interpreter."

He entered.

" Read this letter."

" My adored Henry——"

" Give it me," cried the general: he blew a strong fire from his pipe and consumed it.

5   " Read the other."

" My kind-hearted and beloved son——"

"Stop: read the last line only."

The interpreter answered, "It contains merely the name and address."

10 " I ask no questions: read them, and write them down legibly."

He took the paper, tore off the margin, and placed the line in his snuff-box.

"Give me that paper in pencil, with the mark of 15 sealing-wax on it."

He snatched it, shook some snuff upon it, and shrunk back. It was no sealing-wax; it was a drop of blood: one from the heart,—one only; dry, but seeming fresh.

20 " Read."

" Yes, my dear mother, the greatest name that exists among mortals is that of Sidney. He who now bears it in the front of battle could not succour me. I had advanced too far : I am however no prisoner. Take courage, my too fond mother : I am 25 among the Arabs, who detest the French ; they liberated me. They report, I know not upon what authority, that Bonaparte has deserted his army, and escaped from Egypt."

"Stop instantly," cried Kleber, rising. "Gentlemen," added he to his staff-officers, " my duty 30 obliges me to hear this unbecoming language on

your late commander-in-chief: retire you a few
moments.—Continue."

"He hates every enemy according to his courage and his
virtues: he abominates what he cannot debase, at home or
abroad." 5

"Oh!" whispered Kleber to himself, "he knows
the man so well!"

"The first then are Nelson and Sir Sidney Smith, whose friends
could expect no mercy at his hands. If the report be anything
better than an Arabian tale, I will surrender myself to his suc- 10
cessor as prisoner of war, and perhaps may be soon exchanged.
How will this little leaf reach you? God knows how and when!"

"Is there nothing else to examine?"
"One more leaf."
"Read it." 15

"WRITTEN IN ENGLAND ON THE BATTLE OF ABOUKIR.

"Land of all marvels in all ages past,
  Egypt! I hail thee from a far-off shore;
I hail thee, doom'd to rise again at last,
  And flourish, as in early youth, once more. 20

"How long hast thou lain desolate! how long
  The voice of gladness in thy halls hath ceas'd!
Mute, e'en as Memnon's lyre, the poet's song,
  And half-suppress'd the chant of cloister'd priest.

"Even he, loquacious as a vernal bird, 25
  Love, in thy plains and in thy groves is dumb;
Nor on thy thousand Nile-fed streams is heard
  The reed that whispers happier days to come.

"O'er cities shadowing some dread name divine
  Palace and fane return the hyena's cry, 30
And hoofless camels in long single line
  Stalk slow, with foreheads level to the sky.

" No errant outcast of a lawless isle,
  Mocker of heaven and earth, with vows and prayers,
  Comes thy confiding offspring to beguile,
  And rivet to his wrist the chain he wears.

5   " Britain speaks now : her thunder thou hast heard:
     Conqueror in every land, in every sea ;
     Valour and Truth proclaim the almighty word,
     And, all thou ever hast been, thou shalt be."

" Defender and passionate lover of thy country! "
10 cried Kleber, "thou art less unfortunate than thy
auguries. Enthusiastic Englishman! to which of
your conquests have ever been imparted the benefits
of your laws? Your governors have not even communicated their language to their vassals. Nelson
15 and Sidney are illustrious names: the vilest have
often been preferred to them, and severely have
they been punished for the importunity of their
valour. We Frenchmen have undergone much: but
throughout the whole territory of France, through-
20 out the range of all her new dominions, not a single
man of abilities has been neglected. Remember
this, ye who triumph in our excesses. Ye who
dread our example, speak plainly: is not this among
the examples ye are the least inclined to follow?
25   " Call my staff and a file of soldiers.
     " Gentlemen, he who lies under the pyramid
seems to have possessed a vacant mind and full
heart, qualities unfit for a spy: indeed he was not
one. He was the friend and companion of that
30 Sidney Smith who did all the mischief at Toulon,
when Elliot fled from the city; and who lately, you
must well remember, broke some of our pipes before

Acre—a ceremony which gave us to understand, without the formalities of diplomacy, that the Grand Signor declined the honour of our company to take our coffee with him at Constantinople."

Then turning to the file of soldiers, "A body lies 5 under the Great Pyramid: go, bury it six feet deep. If there is any man among you capable of writing a good epitaph, and such as the brave owe to the brave, he shall have my authority to carve it upon the Great Pyramid; and his name may be brought 10 back to me."

"Allow me the honour," said a lieutenant; "I fly to obey."

"Perhaps," replied the commander-in-chief, "it may not be amiss to know the character, the adven- 15 tures, or at least the name——"

"No matter, no matter, my general."

"Take them, however," said Kleber, holding a copy, "and try your wits."

"General," said Menou, smiling, "you never 20 gave a command more certain to be executed. What a blockhead was that king, whoever he was, who built so enormous a monument for a wandering Englishman!"

Blucher and Sandt.

Blucher. Pardon an intrusion ere sunrise. Do
not move for me.

Sandt. Sir, I was not seated, nor inclined to be.
Sitting is the posture in which a prisoner has a
5 deeper sense of solitude and helplessness. In
walking there is the semblance of being free; and
in standing there is a preparation for walking. But
perhaps these are only the vague ideas of my situation. Many things are true which we do not
10 believe to be true; but more are false which we do
not suspect of falsehood.

Blucher. So early a visit, or indeed any, may be
unwelcome on such a day.

Sandt. To one unprepared it might be. But we
15 are scarcely so early as you think we are. The
walls indeed do not yet bear upon them the pleasant
pink hue of sunrise; a rich decoration which, I am
sorry to think it, some other cells are perhaps
deprived of; but within a few minutes you will
20 discover the only thing in the apartment not yet
visible. Presently you shall see the spider's web,
in the angle there, whiten and wave about. Look!
I told you so. Does the sun's ray shake it by
striking it? Or does the poor laborious weaver of
25 the tissue, by quitting it abruptly?

Blucher. I never thought about the matter.

Sandt. You have not had much leisure then? You never have been idle against your will?

Blucher. No, indeed; not until lately. But why have they walled up your chimney? Could not they have contracted it, if they feared your escape? 5

Sandt. Ah! how we puzzle one another with our questions! Do not inquire why they have done it: thank them rather, if you are my friend, thank them with me for sparing to take down the mantel-piece. 10

Blucher. A narrow slip of lime-washed stone.

Sandt. Wide enough for a cider-glass with a flower in it. I should be unwilling to have a bird so near me just at present; but a flower—I love to have a flower. It leads me back, with its soft, cool 15 touch into the fields and into the garden; it was nurtured by the heavens; it has looked at them in its joyousness; and it leaves all for me! Thou hast been out upon the dew, my little one! thou hast seen everything as I saw it last; thou comest to 20 show me the colours of the dawn, the carelessness of boyhood, the quiet veins and balmy breath of innocence, the brief seclusion and the sound sleep of Sandt.

Are you going? 25

Blucher. No.

Sandt. You turned away from me. I grew tedious.

Blucher. I have not yet given you time, nor you me. What are you looking at on the naked wall? 30

Sandt. I was looking at the reflection of the window-bars against it.

Blucher. And yet you appeared to look at them with pleasure and satisfaction.

Sandt. Did I? Perhaps I did. Their milder apparitions have been my daily visitors. Unob-
5 trusive, calm, consolatory, they teach me by their transiency and evanescence that imprisonment is merely a shadow, as they are; that life is equally so; that the one cannot long detain us; that we cannot long detain the other; and that our enlarge-
10 ment and departure are appointed from above. See how indistinct and how wide-open they are become already. I fell into talking about myself; and, what is worse, I now begin to moralise. An invitation to sit down with one condemned might be
15 offensive.

Blucher. Assure me that I do not offend, and let me assure you I will not be offended. Suspect me, doubt me, interrogate me, and, if you find reason for it, reproach me.

20 *Sandt.* I have no right nor will.

Blucher. Then let us sit together at the foot of the pallet. I would not assume the post of honour, to which I have no right, by taking the three-legged stool. And now we are side by side, may I look at
25 you?

Sandt. As you will.

Blucher. I have seen many brave men; I cannot see too many.

Sandt. The brave are confined in the fortresses—
30 in places less healthy than this. Somebody has misled you.

Blucher. Confined in the fortresses—in places

less healthy than prisons! the landwehr! the re-
storers— Have you slept well? I hope you have;
I do think you have; you look composed.

Sandt. Many thanks! I have indeed.

Blucher. Soundly as usual?   5

Sandt. My sleep was like spring; if inconstant
and fitful, yet kindly and refreshing; such as
becomes the forerunner of a season more settled
and more permanent. It has invigorated me for
the journey I am to take; I wait in readiness.   10

Blucher. Blessings upon you! blessings and glory!

Sandt. Leave me blessings; glory lies within
them: where they are not, she is not.

Blucher. If I tell you that I am one of the same
society with yourself, one of the same heart in its 15
kind, though smaller and harder, you may doubt
me: you may imagine me some privy councillor in
his gentleness come to untwine and wheedle your
secrets out of you; or some literator, in his zeal
for truth, in his affection for science, in his spirit 20
of confraternity, come to catch your words and oil
his salad with them.

Sandt. If you are that (but surely you cannot be)
and poor also, I will answer you enough to produce
you, in this moment of public curiosity, a small 25
pittance for your family.

Blucher. You see I am old, and wear an old coat.

Sandt. Go on. I have given my promise, and
would yet give it, had I not. We have no time to
spare. Let me direct you by the straightest road 30
to your business. I had no accomplice, no instiga-
tor, no adviser in letting fall the acid drop which

removed one stain from Germany. Here is enough for your three volumes, three hundred pages each. Yes, I see the holes; and you may put the hand into that rent.

5 *Blucher.* It is a coat which many a ball has hissed at, and many a courtier whom I cared as little for.

Sandt. May I serve one man more ere I depart! and may he have been, or live to be, an honest one!

Blucher. Is Blucher?

10 *Sandt.* The Kosciusko of Germany, the Washington of Europe.

Blucher. In wishes only.

Sandt. What news about him? Be explicit and expeditious.

15 *Blucher.* He passes yet one hour with thee, O saint without arrogance! O patriot without imposture!

Sandt. Where am I?

Blucher. Not yet in heaven, although thy looks 20 express it.

Sandt. But, what is next to heaven, on earth as I yearned to see it, where the desire of good and the thrusting aside of evil find their full reward.

Blucher. Reward! What! death?

25 *Sandt.* After the embrace of Blucher, are myriads of wrong thoughts worth a single just, or myriads of cruel worth a single kind, one? If men were what we could wish them to be, we need not die for them: if they loved us, we might be too contented, 30 and less disposed to set them right. I dare not attempt to penetrate or to question what is inscrutable in the designs of Providence; but without evil,

and much of it, and spread widely, the highest part
of God's creation would sink lower, by contracting
its capacity of reflection, and abating its intensity
of exertion.

O general, may it be unsafe for any one to pour 5
bad counsel into the ear of princes! Let them
slumber, heavy and satiated, in their sunny
orchards, without the instillation of that fatal
poison! May I not perish, may you not live, in
vain!   10

.   .   .   .   .

Selected Passages.

NATURE.

Demosthenes. Leave to us the country and fresh air, and, what itself is the least tranquil thing in Nature, but is the most potent tranquilliser of an
5 excited soul, the sea.

———

Landor. Ah, Don Pepino! old trees in their living state are the only things that money cannot command. Rivers leave their beds, run into cities, and traverse mountains for it; obelisks and arches,
10 palaces and temples, amphitheatres and pyramids, rise up like exhalations at its bidding; even the free spirit of Man, the only thing great on earth, crouches and cowers in its presence. It passes away and vanishes before venerable trees.

15 ## POETRY.

∨ *Landor.* In poetry, there is a greater difference between the good and the excellent than there is between the bad and the good. Poetry has no golden mean.

———

20 *Landor.* There are some who in a few years can learn all the harmony of Milton; there are others who must go into another state of existence for this felicity.

Normanby. Critics talk most about the *visible* in
sublimity—the Jupiter, the Neptune. Magnitude
and power are sublime but in the second degree,
managed as they may be. Where the heart is not
shaken, the gods thunder and stride in vain. True 5
sublimity is the perfection of the pathetic, which
has other sources' than pity; generosity, for in-
stance, and self-devotion. When the generous and
self-devoted man suffers, there comes pity: the
basis of the sublime is then above the water, and 10
the poet, with or without the gods, can elevate it
above the skies. Terror is but the relic of a child-
ish feeling: pity is not given to children.

FAME.

In another house, after several glasses were 15
drunk with great cheerfulness, the whole company
rose up to a mysterious toast, in silence and sadness. He sipped the wine in doubt, and found that
it was the same as he had been drinking from the
first, and excellent Bordeaux. He could not con- 20
ceive what had saddened at a single moment so
many vacant and rosy faces. The next morning he
heard that two of them had been shot by their
antagonists in a quarrel arising from this toast,—
the "Immortal memory" of some one they had 25
never seen or thought about. He imagined that
silence and sorrow would have come better after;
that wine should make men joyous, and duels
serious. On reflection he feared to be "com-
promised," and suspected that the "immortal 30

memory" so religiously observed, and with such
awe and taciturnity, might be the memory of Bonaparte. To relieve his suspicions, he joked about
it with two of the youngest, whom he found at
5 billiards the succeeding day. They laughed aloud
at his mistake. " It was King William," said one.
"It was William Pitt," said the other. "It was no
more Pitt than it was my pointer," rejoined the
first. In fact the "immortal memory" in eighteen
10 hours had as much obscurity and as many thorns
about it as the tomb of Archimedes.—From *Duke
de Richelieu, Sir Firebrace Cotes, Lady Glengrin, and
Mr. Normanby.*

Barrow. Very wise men, and very wary and in-
15 quisitive, walk over the earth, and are ignorant not
only what minerals lie beneath, but what herbs and
foliage they are treading. Some time afterward,
and probably some distant time, a specimen of ore
is extracted and exhibited; then another; lastly the
20 bearing and diameter of the vein are observed and
measured. Thus it is with writers who are to have
a currency through ages. In the beginning they
are confounded with most others; soon they fall
into some secondary class; next, into one rather
25 less obscure and humble; by degrees they are
liberated from the dross and lumber that hamper
them; and, being once above the heads of contemporaries, rise slowly and waveringly, then regularly
and erectly, then rapidly and majestically, till the
30 vision strains and aches as it pursues them in their
ethereal elevation,

Leontion. The voice comes deepest from the sepulchre, and a great name hath its root in the dead body.

———

Barrow. My dear Newton! the best thing is to stand above the world; the next is to stand apart 5 from it on any side.

SOCIETY.

Penn. Where the lawyers flourish, there is a certain sign that the laws do not.

———

Barrow. There are popes in all creeds, in all 10 countries, in all ages.

———

Odysseus. Believe me, that country will become the most powerful which does the most extensive good. Nations live and remember, when princes have fallen asleep by the side of their fathers, and 15 dynasties have passed away. No princely house was ever grateful long together; a people has a capacious heart, a full one, a sound one, and one that may beat for ages. Oh! who would empoison and paralyse, who would contract and harden, who 20 would estrange and alienate it?

———

Anaxagoras. In most cities, after a time, there are enough of bad citizens to subvert good laws. Immoral life in one leader of the people is more pernicious than a whole street full of impurities in 25 the lower quarters of the community, seeing that streams, foul or fair, cannot flow upward.

TRUTH AND MORALITY.

Peterborough. Penn, I was once a great admirer 5 of Rochefoucauld, and fancied his *Maxims* were oracles. It happened that, quoting them one day at dinner, my adversary told me I had reversed the sentiment; I found I had. Upon this, I began to reverse, for curiosity's sake, almost every third 10 sentence of my shrewd and smart philosopher; and discovered that, like superfine cloth, they look as comely the wrong side outward as the right, wherever I could give as easy and quick a turn as that of the original. This persuaded me that we receive 15 for the wisest things the gracefullest and the boldest, and that what are called speculative truths are in general not only unimportant, but no truths at all.

———

King of Ava. Lovest thou not truth, O Flang- 20 Sarabang-Quang?

Flang. Steel- piercing - questioner - of - prostrate-souls! I am aged. When I was a youth I loved that thing and some others, and found they did me little good. Truth, both in seasons of quiet and 25 of disturbance, raiseth men's anger. One speaks truth to another, and both grow hot; even the silent, whose lungs have not laboured. The rajah or king heareth of it, and he groweth hotter still. They two boil on two sides, he in the centre; but

all boil and foam and bubble, and fume away the
good that is in them.   Now, though I have heard
lies these sixty-five years, I have always found
them productive of complacency.   Some of them
were malignant; yet the malignancy was for the   5
absent; and, supposing he heard of it afterward,
only one could be annoyed where fifty were grati-
fied.   If there is a man in the Celestial Empire who
will lay his hand upon his breast, and declare in the
presence of our gods that he hath derived more 10
pleasure from truth than from lies, then let Kao-
Gong Fao be thrown on his belly, and let his back
be channelled for a bamboo-bed.

Cromwell. Men, like nails, lose their usefulness
when they lose their direction and begin to bend.   15

Dante. Greatness is to goodness what gravel is to
porphyry; the one is a movable accumulation,
swept along the surface of the earth; the other
stands fixed and solid and alone, above the violence
of war and of the tempest, above all that is residu- 20
ous of a wasted world.   Little men build up great
ones; but the snow colossus soon melts.   The
good stand under the eye of God; and therefore
stand.

Jeanne Darc. One hour of self-denial, one hour 25
of stern exertion against the assaults of passion,
outvalues a life of prayer.

THE AFFECTIONS.

Leontion. Never let us think that the time can come when we shall lose our friends. Glory, literature, philosophy have this advantage over friend
5 ship: remove one object from them, and others fill the void; remove one from friendship, one only, and not the earth, nor the universality of worlds, no, nor the intellect that soars above and comprehends them, can replace it!

10 *Princess Mary.* Malice! The baneful word hath shot up from hell in many places, but never between child and parent. In the space of that one span, on that single sod from Paradise, the serpent never trailed. Husband and wife were severed by
15 him, then again clashed together; brother slew brother; but parent and child stand where their Creator first placed them, and drink at the only source of pure, untroubled love.

Filippo Lippi. He inquired of me whether I often
20 thought of those I loved in Italy, and whether I could bring them before my eyes at will. To remove all suspicion from him, I declared I always could, and that one beautiful object occupied all the cells of my brain by night and day. He paused
25 and pondered, and then said, "Thou dost not love deeply." I thought I had given the true signs. "No, Lippi! we who love ardently, we, with all our wishes, all the efforts of our souls, cannot bring be-

fore us the features which, while they were present,
we thought it impossible we ever could forget.
Alas! when we most love the absent, when we most
desire to see her, we try in vain to bring her image
back to us. The troubled heart shakes and con- 5
founds it, even as ruffled waters do with shadows.
Hateful things are more hateful when they haunt
our sleep: the lovely flee away, or are changed into
less lovely."

Cleonè. O Aspasia! it is hard to love, and not 10
to be loved again. I felt it early; I still feel it.
There is a barb beyond the reach of dittany; but
years, as they roll by us, benumb in some degree
our sense of suffering. Season comes after season,
and covers as it were with soil and herbage the 15
flints that have cut us so cruelly in our course.

Messala. From the mysteries of religion the veil
is seldom to be drawn, from the mysteries of love
never. For this offence, the gods take away from
us our freshness of heart and our susceptibility of 20
pure delight. The well loses the spring that fed
it, and what is exposed in the shallow basin soon
evaporates.

SORROW, OLD AGE, AND DEATH.

Epicurus. Pleasures are soon absorbed; they soon 25
evaporate in the heat of youth, and leave no traces
behind them; but sorrows lay waste what they over-

flow, and we have neither time nor art to remove
the obstruction and counteract the sterility.

———

Lucian. The farther we descend into the vale of
years, the fewer illusions accompany us: we have
5 little inclination, little time for jocularity and
laughter. Light things are easily detached from us,
and we shake off heavier as we can. Instead of
levity, we are liable to moroseness: for always near
the grave there are more briars than flowers, unless
10 we plant them ourselves, or our friends supply them.

———

Jeanne Darc. Lady, I am grieved at your sorrow,
although it will hereafter be a source of joy unto
you. The purest water runs from the hardest rock.
Neither worth nor wisdom comes without an effort;
15 and patience and piety and salutary knowledge
spring up and ripen from under the harrow of affliction. Before there is wine or there is oil, the grape
must be trodden and the olive must be pressed.

———

Bossuet. You think it possible that I, aged as I
20 am, may preach a sermon on your funeral. Alas, it
is so! such things have been. There is, however,
no funeral so sad to follow as the funeral of our own
youth, which we have been pampering with fond de-
sires, ambitious hopes, and all the bright berries
25 that hang in poisonous clusters over the path of
life.

Ternissa. Oh, what a thing is age!

Leontion. Death without death's quiet. But we will converse upon it when we know it better.

Epicurus. My beloved! we will converse upon it at the present hour, while the harshness of its fea- 5 tures is indiscernible not only to you, but even to me, who am much nearer to it. Disagreeable things, like disagreeable men, are never to be spoken of when they are present. Do we think, as we may do in such a morning as this, that the air awakens the 10 leaves around us only to fade and perish? Do we, what is certain, think that every note of music we ever heard, every voice that ever breathed into our bosoms and played upon its instrument, the heart, only wafted us on a little nearer to the tomb? Let 15 the idea not sadden, but compose us. Let us yield to it, just as season yields to season, hour to hour; and with a bright serenity, such as Evening is invested with by the departing Sun.

Æsop. Breathe, Rhodopè! breathe again those 20 painless sighs: they belong to thy vernal season. May thy summer of life be calm, thy autumn calmer, and thy winter never come.

Rhodopè. I must die then earlier.

Æsop. Laodameia died; Helen died; Leda, the be- 25 loved of Jupiter, went before. It is better to repose in the earth betimes than to sit up late; better, than to cling pertinaciously to what we feel crumbling under us, and to protract an inevitable fall. We may enjoy the present while we are insensible of in- 30 firmity and decay: but the present, like a note in music, is nothing but as it appertains to what is past and what is to come. There are no fields of amaranth on this side of the grave; there are no voices, 5 O Rhodopè, that are not soon mute, however tuneful; there is no name, with whatever emphasis of passionate love repeated, of which the echo is not faint at last.

Rhodopè. O Æsop! let me rest my head on yours; 10 it throbs and pains me.

Æsop. What are these ideas to thee?

Rhodopè. Sad, sorrowful.

Æsop. Harrows that break the soil, preparing it for wisdom. Many flowers must perish ere a grain 15 of corn be ripened.

NOTES.

ÆSOP AND RHODOPÈ (1846).

This is the second of two conversations between the same characters. All these conversations, it must be remembered, are imaginary, even the story of the famine in the present one being a pure invention of Landor's. It is therefore frequently idle to search in history or legend for scenes and dates. The assumed scene of this conversation, as may be learned from its predecessor and from at least one local touch in itself, is Egypt. *Rhodo'pis* (" Rosy-cheek "—Landor employs a musical variant, *Rhod'opè*, also a Thracian name) was the appellative of a Thracian slave girl whose real name was probably Doricha ; see Herodotus, ii. 134, 135 ; Strabo, xvii. 33. Herodotus says that she and Æsop were fellow-slaves of Iadmon of Samos, whence she was afterward taken by Xanthes (Xanthus) to Egypt. Landor makes them meet first in Egypt, though there is no evidence that Æsop ever visited that country, either as slave or as freedman. This is of course the Æsop who lived about 570 B. C. and to whom is attributed, on very uncertain grounds, a body of familiar Greek fables. The relative ages of the two can be gathered from the conversation, and upon the age of Rhodopè might well turn some criticism of dramatic consistency. It is needful to know that Landor accepts both the tradition of Rhodopè's great beauty, which passed into a proverb, and the unwarrantable and unreasonable tradition of Æsop's physical ugliness.

I : 22.—*For I have looked into nothing else of late.* Readers of Landor must early acquaint themselves with his implicit style. This clause might seem to mean that Æsop has been pondering deeply upon the possibility of Rhodopè's doing wrong. But such an interpretation would be fatally prosaic. The moment we discover the exact allusion in " nothing else," we discover the full significance of Æsop's delicate implication.

2 : 6.—*Curiosity.* In the first conversation Æsop had teasingly convicted Rhodopè of this " feminine appurtenance."

2 : 11.—*Cover thy face.* See Introduction, p. xxvii. There are several other such disguised indications of the action.

3 : 23.—*Could any other?* Supply the noun. Is it the father's insensibility or the daughter's worth that is uppermost in Æsop's mind? And what is the reference below in "intolerable wretchedness"?

4 : 3.—*Is it,* etc. Note where the sentence-stress falls.

4 : 32.—*Beanfield.* Whether Landor is thinking of the Pythagorean bean (*Nelumbo*) and confounding it with the Homeric lotos is of small consequence—Æsop's little parable is not hard to interpret. Indeed, readers who like to analyse the sources of their pleasure will find that this paragraph subserves at least three highly artistic ends.

7 : 27.—*Every one had bought.* Does Rhodopè state this as simple fact?

11 : 4.—*Midas,* type of avarice ; *Lycaon,* of inhumanity.

12 : 8.—*Rhæsus.* Properly *Rhesus.* Selected here, because a Thracian hero.

12 : 17.—*Pardon me.* Why this deprecation? Recall the origin of the Trojan war.

12 : 24.—*The Fates also have sung.* Prophetic of the event in the life of Rhodopis which is told by Strabo and by Ælian, and which suggests the story of Cinderella. While she was bathing, an eagle caught up one of her sandals and bearing it to Memphis dropped it in the lap of the king, Psammetichus, who was moved by the strange occurrence and the beauty of the sandal to send out messengers in search of the owner. " They, finding Rhodopis at Naucratis, brought her to Egypt, where the king wedded her ; and after her death she was buried under the pyramid that goes by her name."

Trace the successive impressions left upon the reader in regard to Rhodopè's father, and note the heightening of dramatic interest. What turns out to be the final and supreme justification of his act?

NOTES. 151

What story runs through the whole conversation, or sometimes like an undercurrent, beneath it? May not the closing paragraph be regarded as the conclusion, or a revised conclusion, of the broken speech of Æsop toward the beginning?

MARCELLUS AND HANNIBAL (1828).

The characters here are Marcus Claudius Marcellus, five times Roman consul, and conqueror of Syracuse ; and Hannibal, the great Carthaginian general. The death of the former in the defeat near Venusia—208 B. C., second Punic war—is recorded history. Recorded too are the stories of the ring and the funeral. " When Hannibal came up to the body," says Appian (*Hannib.*, 50), "and saw the wounds all in the breast, he praised him as a soldier but accounted him a bad general ; and after securing his seal-ring he gave the body an honourable funeral and sent the ashes to the dead man's son in the Roman camp." Compare Plutarch, *Marcellus*, 30. But the conversation is no less imaginary than the preceding, since it does not appear from history that Marcellus survived until the arrival of his conqueror. The conception, however, is a happy one, and the execution so perfect that we rise with the development of the situation to the level of the heroism portrayed.

15 : 1.—*No faster.* What does Hannibal mean?

15 : 11. — *The Romans, too.* The whole story of the Carthaginian campaign lies behind this word *too.* There is authentic history also behind the speech that follows.

17 : 12.—*It pains me.* Follow carefully the motives that prompt these speeches.

17 : 29.— *This ring.* Probably suggesting massiveness? Livy (xxvii. 23) tells that Hannibal, by the use of a letter sealed with this ring, secured the admission of six hundred of his men into the town of Salapia, Apulia. But the Salapians had been apprised of the trick and ambushed the men.

18 : 7.—*I confess.* This sentence seems to have no direct connection with the preceding, which looks backward while this looks forward. Such sudden shifting of thought is characteristic of Landor's dramatic style. The shift in this case, however, turns

out to be merely a resumption. The conversation had for a moment diverged.

20 : 1.—*Bubbles of air.* Air, breath, life, and spirit were represented in Latin by a single word—*spiritus.* *Piety* below keeps also its older meaning.

20 : 28.—*He would have* Force of *would?*

Is Hannibal here represented as noble and generous, or only selfish and cunning?

What principle, in this and other conversations, seems to govern Landor in the use of the second personal pronoun, now in the solemn form *thou,* and now in the common form *you?*

P. SCIPIO ÆMILIANUS, POLYBIUS, PANÆTIUS (1833).

After a terrible siege in which her inhabitants were reduced from seven hundred thousand to fifty thousand, in 146 B. C., the chapter of history which the illustrious city of Carthage had been writing for seven hundred years was brought to a sad close. The third Punic war is perhaps the greatest blot on Roman history. The senate decreed, and their instrument, Scipio Africanus the Younger, could do no less than perform. The city was besieged and razed with Roman rigour and Stoic fortitude, though not, if Landor has read this character aright, without some human heart-ache. Cicero raised a monument to the memory of Scipio by making his friendship with Lælius the inspiration of the beautiful dialogue *De Amicitia.* Landor has added a scarcely less beautiful tribute in this scene which brings Scipio himself before our eyes in tender and intimate converse with his Greek friends, Polybius the historian and Panætius the Stoic philosopher. Only the opening pages are given here of a conversation which runs to considerable length, treating discursively of various things, chiefly of luxury and the debt of Rome to Greece. The interest centres in the vivid presentation of a complex character, the product of Roman birth and military training humanised by Greek philosophy and culture.

23 : 14.—*Rome be what Carthage was* "And they say that Scipio was heard mourning, *The day shall come when sacred Ilion will fall, and Priam, and the people of Priam.* And when

Polybius asked him of what he was thinking, he made answer as one in abstraction, *Rome.*"—APPIAN, *Lib.* 132.

24 : 32.—*His wife none.* Asdrubal, says Appian (*Lib.* 131), fled with his two boys to surrender to Scipio. But his wife reproached him for a traitor, slew the children, and threw them and herself into the fire.

METELLUS AND MARIUS (1829).

" Marius was young at the siege of Numantia, and, entering the army with no advantage of connection, would have risen slowly ; but Scipio had marked his regularity and good morals, and desirous of showing the value he placed on discipline, when he was asked who, in case of accident to him, should succeed to the chief command, replied, *Perhaps this man*, touching the shoulder of Marius." LANDOR's note, after Plutarch, *Marius*, 3.

From his obscurity Marius rose to be seven times consul, and by his rivalry with Sulla brought on the civil war of 88 and the consequent proscription and slaughter of the nobles. Caius Cæcilius Metellus was a comparatively unimportant personage. The siege and capture, in 132 B. C., of the gallant Numantians, hopelessly struggling with eight thousand men against the whole power of Rome, was another disgraceful stage in the Roman career of conquest at which Scipio found it his duty to assist. Appian (*Iber.*, 95-98) says that some of the Numantians preferred surrender to death and were led in a Roman triumph. The fundamental conception, therefore, in this dramatic scene, as well as many details, is Landor's own, and is a pure triumph of the creative imagination working upon a few suggestions from history.

26 : 20.—*I should slip else.* The awful significance of Marius's words will not escape the reader as it escapes Metellus.

27 : 6.—*Cereate.* The rustic home of Marius's childhood, near Arpinum. A good example of how Landor makes every touch tell. For the simile compare page 125, line 14.

31 : 1.—*Auguries are surer.* " This saying of Scipio's [see Landor's note above], we are told, raised the hopes of Marius like a divine oracle, and was the chief thing which animated him to apply himself to affairs of state."—PLUTARCH.

LUCULLUS AND CÆSAR (1829).

"It is difficult to gather from this conversation the date at which it is supposed to take place; probably it is not possible to do so. Cæsar has come to visit Lucullus in secret, to ask him for his help against Pompey. At no time would Cæsar have been likely to take such a step, least of all during the full tide of his success in Gaul, when his alliance with Pompey was still vigorous. But the history is unimportant. For the splendours of the villa of Lucullus, see Plutarch's *Life of Lucullus*, which has furnished Landor with the materials for his picture."—G. G. CRUMP.

An allusion, in a part of the conversation not here reprinted, to the consuls Gabinius and Piso makes it clear that Landor had in mind the date, 58 B. C. This agrees with other allusions,—to the marriage of Julia, to the affair of Vettius, to Cæsar's impending departure for Gaul. Some minor matters, however, are not quite reconcilable. The season is "the dog-days," when Cæsar must have been in Gaul, whither he went early in the spring. Perhaps we are to imagine him as having slipped back into Italy, where as imperator he had no right to be, and as having made his way to Lucullus's villa, "avoiding the cities." But Mr. Crump is right in pointing out the improbability of Cæsar's approaching Lucullus at this early stage of the "first triumvirate."

The villa of Lucullus was near Tusculum, ten miles southeast of Rome. Lucullus, after withdrawing from public affairs,—virtually forced out by the success of Pompey, his old rival, and Cæsar,—devoted himself to a life of philosophic indolence and luxury, made possible by the vast wealth amassed in his wars against Mithridates, King of Pontus. He died about 57 B. C. Landor supposes him to have been slowly poisoned.

The notable features of the conversation are the craft and diplomacy lurking beneath the veil of friendliness and hospitality, the delicious sparring in which the honours are all on one side and the ultimate triumph of the magnanimity of Lucullus, in whom it is impossible not to see a man much after Landor's own heart.

33 : 15.— *That worthy.* The probability is that this "worthy,"

Vettius by name, was suborned by one of Cæsar's own party to make this false charge, that it might redound to the injury of Cicero, Lucullus, and others. Such was Cicero's belief, shared also, in Landor's view, by Lucullus, beneath the irony of whose next speech here Cæsar palpably winces.

34 : 12.—*Formian wine.* Readers of Horace will remember that in one of his Odes (i. 20) he hints to his patron that he cannot afford Falernian and Formian wines.

34 : 20.—*Pardons heavier faults.* That the conqueror of Gaul should endure calmly the infliction of such exquisite torture is almost beyond comprehension. But Landor's characters, unless they be kings, are not to be expected to descend to violence.

36 : 30.—*Cherries.* " Blessings on Lucullus !" Horatius is made to exclaim in another conversation, " the wisest and most provident of conquerors. He brought from Armenia the apricot and cherry, and the peach from the confines of Persia."—*Lake Larius,* now *Como.*

37 : 26.—*Fiesulæ.* The Italian *Fiesole,* which became Landor's home the year in which this conversation was published.

38 : 9.—*Does it now appear.* Several late editions read " does not now appear "—a reading which will also bear interpretation. It is difficult to choose between them.

38 : 32.—*Contests in the Senate.* Cato, leader of the aristocracy, opposed Cæsar and Pompey.

39 : 5.—*On the ceiling.* It is to be remembered that the Romans reclined at banquets.

40 : 1.—*The subject.* In his youth Cæsar had once been captured by pirates. He was ransomed, but laughingly threatened to crucify them. He afterward manned some vessels, captured the pirates, and carried out the threat. Landor was much interested in pictures, of which he was a collector, though scarcely a connoisseur.

43 : 2.—*Virtues.* Here follows Cæsar's direct request of Lucullus to unite with him against Pompey and Crassus. How the request is met the remainder of the scene as here printed shows.

44 : 21.—*Will tread down the sandal.* A low estimate of Cicero, who at this date was still alive;—carrying out the idea that no man is rightly estimated before his death.

TIBERIUS AND VIPSANIA (1828).

" Vipsania, the daughter of Agrippa, was divorced from Tiberius by Augustus and Livia, in order that he might marry Julia
and hold the empire by inheritance. He retained such an affection for her, and showed it so intensely when he once met her
afterwards, that every precaution was taken lest they should meet
again."—LANDOR's note, after Suetonius, *Tiberius,* vii.

Tiberius Claudius Nero, the second Emperor of Rome, born
B. C. 42, was the son of Livia Drusilla, who afterward became
the wife of Augustus, first emperor of Rome. He was carefully
educated; was sent by Augustus in the year 20 on an expedition
into Armenia and visited the island of Rhodes on his return; was
divorced in 11 from Vipsania and married to Julia, the daughter of
Augustus; spent the years 6 B. C. to 2 A. D. in Rhodes; was
adopted by Augustus 4 A. D; reigned 14-37 A. D. The mention
of the " Little Drusus " indicates that the time of this conversation is assumed to be before the second visit to Rhodes, therefore
between 11 and 6 B. C. The following table of genealogy will be
of assistance:

$$\text{Agrippa} \qquad \text{Livia (3)} = \text{(2) Augustus}$$
$$|\qquad\qquad\qquad |\qquad\qquad\qquad |$$
$$\text{Vipsania (1)} = \text{Tiberius} = \text{(2) Julia}$$
$$|$$
$$\text{Drusus}$$

Landor's conception of Tiberius is scarcely the historical one,
but in another conversation (*Marchese Pallavicini and Walter
Landor*) he has this defence of it: " Tiberius, melancholy
at the loss of a young and beautiful wife borne away from
him by policy, sank into that dreadful malady which blighted
every branch of the Claudian family; and, instead of embellishing
the city with edifices and sculpture, darkened it with disquietudes
and suspicions, and retired into a solitude which his enemies have
peopled with monsters. Such atrocious lust, incredible even in
madness itself, was incompatible with the memory of his loss and
with the tenderness of his grief." The entire conversation is

tense with passion and broken and elliptical, leaving much exercise for the imagination in supplying the action of the speakers
and in following the vacillating, or rather oscillating, temper of
Tiberius. Mr. Swinburne praises it as an exhibition of Landor's
" subtle and sublime and terrible power to enter the dark vesti-
bule of distraction, to throw the whole force of his fancy, the
whole fire of his spirit, into the ' shadowing passion ' (as Shakespeare calls it) of gradually imminent insanity." But Mr. Swinburne is neither the first nor the last person to discover in it one
of the few supreme triumphs of the creative imagination working
in the field of dramatic art.

51 : 32.—*I cursed then audibly.* " I cursed them audibly " is
a common, but manifestly erroneous, reading.

WOLFGANG AND HENRY OF MELCTAL (1828).

" Landenberg, who governed the country for Albert of Austria,
sent to drive away a yoke of oxen from Henry of Melctal. His
son Arnold, complaining of the violence, was told that *peasants
might draw the plough themselves if they wanted bread.* Arnold
struck him with his staff, broke two fingers, and fled to a friend
at Uri. On this, the father, in his extreme old age, saw his
cattle driven from his farm, his goods confiscated, his house
seized,—and nothing else; for his eyes were burned out."—
LANDOR'S note.

Arnold von Melchthal, of the Swiss canton of Unterwalden,
son of the Henry of this conversation, was one of three heroic
mountaineers who about 1307 conspired to deliver the Three
Forest Cantons from the yoke of Albert of Austria. Into the
probably real incident has become woven the legendary story of
" William Tell," and Arnold is a prominent character in Schil-
ler's drama, " Wilhelm Tell." Landor has put into this conversation his hatred of imperial power and his sympathy with
the human instinct for freedom. The portion omitted contains a
" seditious song " which the young Arnold is accused of having
composed and sung.

SOUTHEY AND LANDOR (1846).

The friendship between Landor and Southey began in 1808. " I never saw any one," Southey wrote of the first meeting, " more unlike myself in every prominent part of human charac- ter, nor any one who so cordially and instinctively agreed with me on so many of the most important subjects." The friendship was broken only by Southey's death, thirty-five years afterward. It was kept up chiefly by correspondence, yet such a conversation as the present one may not have been even in small part imaginary; in fact, this is represented as having taken place near Clifton, where Southey visited Landor in 1836 or 1837. For the character and value of Landor's literary criticism, see Introduction, page xlii. The present criticism is intentionally conducted, according to the opening of the dialogue, " not incidentally, but turning page after page "; for which Landor's quaint defence is: " It would ill become us to treat Milton with generalities. Radishes and salt are the *picnic* quota of slim spruce reviewers ! Let us hope to find somewhat more solid and of better taste."

63 : 4 —*Cose non dette.* The line is inexactly quoted, no doubt from memory. See *Orlando Furioso*, i, 2, 2.

ANDREW MARVEL AND BISHOP PARKER (1846).

" He [Parker] wrote a work entitled, as Hooker's was, *Ecclesi- astical Polity*, in which are these words: ' It is better to submit to the unreasonable impositions of Nero and Caligula than to hazard the dissolution of the State. . . Princes may with less danger give liberty to men's vices and debaucheries than to their consciences.' Marvel answered him in his *Rehearsal Transprosed*, in which he says of Milton: ' I well remember that, being one day at his house, I there first met you, and accidentally. Then it was that you wandered up and down Moorfields, astrologising upon the duration of His Majesty's Government. You frequented John Milton incessantly, and haunted his house day by day. What discourses you there used he is too generous to remember, but, he

never having in the least provoked you, it is inhumanely and in-
hospitably done to insult thus over his old age. I hope it will be
a warning to all others, as it is to me, to avoid, I will not say such
a Judas, but a man that creeps into all companies, to jeer, trepan,
and betray them.' "—LANDOR's note.

Andrew Marvel, or rather Marvell, the poet, found a friend
and helper in the greater poet Milton, and became Assistant Latin
Secretary with him in the last years of Cromwell's Protectorate.
He was a staunch Puritan, continuing after the Restoration
to be fearlessly outspoken against abuses in Church and State.
Landor has introduced him as interlocutor in four other conversations, in three of them with Milton. Landor admired both characters for their intrepid patriotism and their hatred of popery and
prelaty, and the spectacle here presented of Marvell so eloquently
defending his aged and fallen patron must move the most un-
sympathetic of readers. As for Samuel Parker, he was " one of
the worst specimens of the highest of high churchmen of the reign
of Charles II."

The conversation must be assumed to have taken place some
time after the Restoration and after the publication of Milton's
Paradise Lost (1667). Marvell's commendatory verses, alluded to
in the beginning, are found prefixed only to the second edition of
Paradise Lost (1674), so that if Landor were particular about ac-
curacy we should have to fix the date in the very last year of Milton's life. Moreover, 1672 is the date of the beginning of the
controversy between Marvell and Parker. The entire conversation, less than one-fourth of which is here reprinted, is pitched in
a lofty key. That Parker was not made bishop till after Marvell's
death, that a conversation in this strain is improbable, that full
justice is not done to all sides of Marvell's lively wit, count for
little or nothing; the imaginative achievement remains. It may
well be doubted whether English prose of the nineteenth century
can show anything to equal, for exalted dignity and sustained
power, the utterances that Landor has put into Marvell's mouth—
the utterances of a profound nature profoundly stirred, in which
truth is irradiated by terrible beauty, and wrath, justified by the
righteousness of its cause, lifts satire itself to the level of the
sublime.

73 : 2.—*Power . . . glory.* Which of these words Landor means to be understood in a derogatory sense may not be at once clear. But in another conversation he makes Marvell console Henry Marten in his imprisonment because the privilege of a " memory, justly proud," is still his: "Hast thou not sat convivially with Oliver Cromwell? Hast thou not conversed familiarly with the only man greater than he, John Milton? One was ambitious of perishable power, the other of imperishable glory; both have attained their aim."

75 : 24.—*Etna.* See *Empedocles,* Classical Dictionary; or Matthew Arnold's poem, *Empedocles on Etna.*—*Grotto del Cane.* In this "grotto of the dog," near Naples, carbonic-acid gas collects near the floor in sufficient quantity to kill an animal.

80 : 1.—*Bridewell logwood.* The general meaning is clear: Men of meaner, though perhaps showier, talent have been preferred to Milton. But the specific allusion, if there be one, is obscure. Logwood, used both in dyeing, and in medicine as an astringent, is prepared for the trade, probably by prison labour, in the form of chips and raspings. The allusion, then, may be to the style of meaner writers. In another conversation, Southey is made to say: " As some men conceive that, if their name is engraven in Gothic letters with several superfluous, it denotes antiquity of family, so do others that a congestion of words swept together out of a corner, and dry chopped sentences which turn the mouth awry in reading, make them look like original thinkers. Milton is none of these; and his language is never a patchwork."

The rhythm and cadence of Landor's sentences can be better studied, perhaps, in this selection than in any other. The flood of Marvell's eloquence is not without its eddies, rapids, and falls, but in general the torrent sweeps steadily on, and every boulder the bishop can throw into it is swallowed up without diminishing its force or materially deflecting its current.

ESSEX AND SPENSER (1834).

Spenser went to Ireland as secretary to Lord Grey, the Lord-Deputy, where he was finally given a grant of land, the manor and castle of Kilcolman, near the Awbeg (the " aldered Mulla " of his poems) in the county of Cork. Late in 1598, during the rebellion of Tyrone, fire was set to the castle, and Spenser had to flee with his wife Elizabeth and their little children to England. That a child perished in the flames is regarded now as pure myth, resting only on a statement ascribed to Ben Jonson by Drummond of Hawthornden. Spenser died at London in January, 1599, possibly in poverty, though Essex, the queen's favourite, just then appointed to the disastrous lord-lieutenancy of Ireland, may well have befriended him.

90 : 27.—*Acorns from Penshurst.* Penshurst, in Kent, was the home of Sir Philip Sidney, whose friendship for Spenser, like his uncle Leicester's and Sir Walter Raleigh's, both does credit to himself and lends lustre to the life of the poet. Sidney was killed at the battle of Zutphen, in the Netherlands, 1586; Essex married his widow in 1590. " Sidney's Oak, a gnarled and broken monarch, planted at his birth," may still be seen in the park at Penshurst Place.

92 : 18.—*None to save thee ?*

> Was there no star that could be sent,
> No watcher in the firmament,
> No angel from the countless host
> That loiters round the crystal coast,
> Could stoop to heal that only child?
> —EMERSON: *Threnody.*

94 : 20.—*Even like one not powerful.* " Now for the first time I learn that any great power hath been exerted for any great good."—LANDOR: *Chaucer, Boccaccio, and Petrarca.*

95 : 6.—*Guardian angels.* See the two beautiful stanzas at the beginning of the eighth canto of the second book of the *Faërie Queene.*

THE LADY LISLE AND ELIZABETH GAUNT (1826).

" Burnet relates from William Penn, who was present, that Elizabeth Gaunt placed the fagots round her body with her own hands. Lady Lisle was not burned alive, though sentenced to it; but hanged and beheaded."—LANDOR's note.

The time is 1685, shortly after the accession of James II., when so many of the sympathisers with Monmouth's rising were tried and executed during the famous " Bloody Circuit " of Lord Jeffreys, Chief Justice. Alice, widow of the regicide John Lisle (their title came only from Cromwell), harboured in her house John Hickes, a Nonconformist divine, and another man, chiefly out of kindness, as she had before befriended cavaliers. Elizabeth Gaunt was convicted on the testimony of the very man, one James Burton, whom she had shielded at the time of the Rye House Plot. See Macaulay's History, vol. i. The two women could not have met, as they were executed at different times and in different places.

97 : 31.—*Forbidden it.* The first edition adds, " We must bend to the authority of both; but first to the earlier, and most willingly to the better." This is only one of many examples of Landor's constant effort for conciseness, and shows well how he sacrificed popularity to the ideals of his art. For it is clear in this place that he did not wish, in expunging the sentence, to expunge the thought. But the thought is in the nature of argument, and in dramatic and poetic composition argument is better implied than expressed. Landor prefers, therefore, to take his chances with the reader. And for the reader who is alert and sympathetic enough to supply the ellipsis, the gain is very great, but it is doubtful whether many would supply it without the knowledge of what was originally written.

THE EMPRESS CATHARINE AND PRINCESS DASHKOF (1829).

Catharine was not present at the murder of her husband, if he was murdered; " nor is it easy to believe that Clytemnestra was at the murder of hers," wrote Landor; " our business is character." Even this business, it is well to remember, involves much imagination and employs great license; few will believe that Landor has not overdrawn his character of Catharine. Peter III.

died at Ropsha, fifteen miles from Peterhof, in 1762. It is probable that he was strangled by one of the brothers Orloff, favourites of Catharine, and that she abetted the design, which placed her upon the throne. Ivan the Sixth, a weakling who had reigned a short time in his infancy, some twenty years before, was now kept imprisoned, and after two years slain, ostensibly to prevent his deliverance by one Mirovitch, lieutenant of the guards. Mirovitch's life was also forfeited. See Rambaud, *Hist. of Russia*, vol. ii. The Princess Dashkof left memoirs of the time. Voltaire celebrated Catharine as the Semiramis of the North. A good companion-piece to this conversation is *Peter the Great and Alexis*, in which, however, Landor's portraiture of Peter the Great becomes almost travesty.

102 : 14.—*A whale.* The vast extent of the Russian empire and the conglomerate character of her people, from Poles and Finns to Cossacks and Tartars, had evidently made a deep impression upon Landor's imagination. Elsewhere he likens her to " a great lobster or crab, strong both in the body and claws; but between the body and claws there is a part easy to be severed and broken." Again, " Her empire will split and splinter into the infinitesimals of which its vast shapeless body is composed. The south breathes against it, and it dissolves."

105 : 24.—*Pantaloons and facings.* " The reforms that he introduced into the dress and drill, so as to assimilate them to those of Prussia, irritated the army."—RAMBAUD.

106 : 22.—*Frederick's.* Voltaire went to live in Prussia at the request of Frederick the Great, but after several years they parted enemies. Voltaire's poem, *La Pucelle*, mentioned in the next line, is a coarse, burlesque performance.

108 : 17.—*Men in general.* Compare the following sentiment, from the dialogue between Louis Bonaparte and Count Molé : " *Louis Bonaparte.* But honour is left at the bottom of the heart. *Count Molé.* If not there, yet under it, on the same side. The scabbard holds it."

108 : 32.—*Paphos or Tobolsk.* That is, they must choose between the shrine of love and exile.

LEOFRIC AND GODIVA (1829).

This legend of Coventry, where the festival of Godiva is still celebrated, belongs to the middle of the eleventh century. Leofric was an earl of Mercia, whose earldom included the present county of Warwick, Landor's native shire. The beauty of the conversation has been universally praised. It must rank among the very best of Landor's short, less impassioned dialogues, as the *Epicurus, Leontion, and Ternissa*, his own especial favourite, must rank among the longer ones.

114 : 22.—*Unsparingly.* First edition reads "abundantly." Evidently the change was made to avoid any suspicion of euphuistic balance. See Introduction, page xlvii. So, a few lines below, "sustenance" has replaced the original word "food," doubtless to eliminate a rhyme.

VITTORIA COLONNA AND MICHEL-ANGELO BUONARROTI (1846).

Vittoria Colonna, widow of the Italian general Marchese di Pescara, was through the last ten years of her life a prominent figure in a celebrated circle of Roman artists, poets, and religious reformers. She composed some beautiful sonnets to the memory of her husband. Michel-Angelo's friendship with her began when he was about sixty years of age, and some of his later sonnets were inspired by and addressed to her. A conversation between them was recorded by Francesco D'Ollanda. See Grimm's *Life of Michel-Angelo*, chapter xiv.

GENERAL KLÉBER AND FRENCH OFFICERS (1824).

Napoleon, including the East in his schemes of conquest, won the battle of the Pyramids over the Mamelukes in 1798, though his fleet was destroyed by Nelson in the battle of the Nile. Attempting next the subjugation of Syria, he was met by the armies of the Turkish Sultan, and at Acre he was forced to retreat, partly through the gallant action of Sir Sidney Smith, an English cap-

tain who had been with Hood at Toulon in 1793, and who now
rushed to the relief of the Turks. Returning to Egypt, he won
a victory over fifteen thousand Turks at Abukir in 1799, and then
sailed for France, transferring the Egyptian command to General
Kléber. Kléber was an able commander and a worthy man, but
he was assassinated the next year, and the command devolved
upon the incompetent Menou, under whom the French armies
speedily met disaster.

" I have been told," wrote Julius Hare in 1827, " that among
Landor's *Conversations* the most general favourite is that between
General Kléber and some French officers." This was before the
strongest dramatic scenes had been published. Landor often introduced narrative into his dialogues; here we have dialogue set
in narrative. The effect is at least so good that we could wish he
had tried it more frequently. In reading this, some allowance
must be made for his hatred of the French and of Napoleon in
particular.

BLÜCHER AND SANDT (1846).

The famous Prussian field-marshal, Blücher, needs no charac-
terisation. Karl Ludwig Sand, or Sandt, was a German student
and liberal who, inflamed by the endeavours of the ruling princes
to suppress all revolutionary sentiments, sought out and stabbed
at Mannheim August von Kotzebue, the German dramatist, then
in the secret service of the Russian Czar. Landor has constructed
one of his dialogues, *Sandt and Kotzebue*, with this assassination
as a climax. The present dialogue, it seems clear from some portions here omitted, is assumed to have taken place before the final
downfall of Napoleon. It therefore involves an anachronism, for
Sandt's crime, imprisonment, and execution belong to the years
1819-20. The diction of the dialogue is in one or two places not
quite up to Landor's standard of purity.

SELECTED PASSAGES.

These detached passages have been included both for their own
value and to show what selections of separate excellence may be

made from almost any of the *Conversations*, so often in their entirety laborious to read. A few only have been admitted, and these, even after Mr. Colvin's example, with much hesitation, for the common aversion to extracts is grounded in reason. Still, there are writers of whom we can fairly make an exception. There are those whose writings have been chiefly in the nature of inconsecutive thoughts, like Marcus Aurelius and Emerson; and there are those whose best utterances have such completeness, such breadth of application, and such individual perfection of form that their value is not seriously impaired by detachment from the context—among whom we can have no hesitation in ranking Landor.

ENGLISH READINGS

16mo, cloth. Prices net

PROSE

Addison: Selections. Edited by EDWARD B. REED, Assistant Professor in Yale University. xxxii+360 pp. 80 cents.

Arnold: Prose Selections. Edited, with notes and an introduction, by LEWIS E. GATES, sometime Professor in Harvard College. xci+348 pp. 75 cents.

Burke: On Conciliation. Edited, with introduction and notes, by DANIEL V. THOMPSON, Teacher in the Lawrenceville School. xliv+122 pp. 30 cents.

Burke: Selections. Chosen, and edited with a full introduction, by BLISS PERRY, Editor of *Atlantic Monthly.* xxvi+298 pp. 75 cents.

Coleridge: Prose Selections. Selections chosen, and edited with introduction and notes, by HENRY A. BEERS, Professor in Yale University. xxix+146 pp. 50 cents.

De Quincey: The English Mail Coach and Joan of Arc. With an introduction and notes by JAMES MORGAN HART, Professor in Cornell University. xxvi+138 pp. 50 cents.

Dryden: Essays on the Drama. Edited by WILLIAM STRUNK, Jr., Assistant Professor in Cornell University. xxxviii+180 pp. 60 cents.

Johnson: Selections. Edited by C. G. OSGOOD, Preceptor in Princeton University. lx+479 pp. 90 cents.

Johnson: Rasselas. With an introduction and notes by OLIVER FARRAR EMERSON, Professor in Western Reserve University. lv+179 pp. 50 cents.

Landor: Selections from the Imaginary Conversations. Edited by. ALPHONSO G. NEWCOMER, Professor in Leland Stanford University. lix+166 pp. 60 cents.

Macaulay: Essays on Milton and Addison. Edited, with notes, by JAMES ARTHUR TUFTS, Professor in the Phillips Exeter Academy. xlix+226 pp. 35 cents.

Macaulay and Carlyle: Croker's Boswell's Johnson. The complete essays, with brief notes and an introduction by W. STRUNK, Jr., Assistant Professor in Cornell University. With portrait of Johnson on his tour through the Hebrides. xl+192 pp. 50 cents.

Nettleton's Old Testament Narratives. Selected and edited, with an introduction, by George H. NETTLETON, Ph.D., Assistant Professor in Yale University. xxxvii+294 pp. 60 cents.

Newman: Prose Selections. Edited, with introduction and notes, by LEWIS E. GATES, sometime Professor in Harvard University. lxi+228 pp. 75 cents.

Pater: Prose Selections. Edited by E. E. HALE, Professor in Union College. lxxvi+208 pp. 75 cents.

Poe: Selections from his Critical Writings. Edited by F. C. PRESCOTT, Assistant Professor in Cornell University. li+348 pp. 75 cents.

Ruskin: Sesame and Lilies. Edited, with an introduction and notes, by ROBERT K. ROOT, Ph.D., Preceptor in Princeton University. xxviii+137 pp. 35 cents.

Swift: Prose Selections. Edited by FREDERICK C. PRESCOTT, Assistant Professor in Cornell University. xliii+229 pp. 75 cents.

Thackeray: English Humourists. Edited, with an introduction and notes, by WILLIAM LYON PHELPS, Professor of English Literature in Yale University. xii+360 pp. 80 cents.

FORMS OF DISCOURSE

Andrews's Specimens of Discourse. Selected and edited by ARTHUR L. ANDREWS, Instructor in Cornell University. v+289 pp. 60 cents.

Baker's Specimens of Argumentation. Chosen and edited by GEORGE P. BAKER, Professor in Harvard University. 186 pp. 50 cents.

Baldwin's Specimens of Prose Description. Edited, with introduction and notes, by CHARLES SEARS BALDWIN, Ph.D., Professor in Yale University. l+149 pp. 50 cents.

Bouton's The Lincoln-Douglas Debates. Edited by A. L. BOUTON, Assistant Professor in New York University. v+297 pp. 60 cents.

Brewster's Specimens of Prose Narration. Chosen and edited by WILLIAM T. BREWSTER, Assistant Professor in Columbia University. xxxvii+209 pp. 90 cents.

Lamont's Specimens of Exposition. Selected and edited by HAMMOND LAMONT, formerly Professor in Brown University. xxx+180 pp. 50 cents.

Lewis's Specimens of the Forms of Discourse. By EDWIN HERBERT LEWIS, Professor in Lewis Institute, Chicago. viii+367 pp. 60 cents.

Nettleton's Specimens of the Short Story. Selected and edited by GEORGE H. NETTLETON, Ph.D., Assistant Professor in Yale University. vii+229 pp. 50 cents.

POETRY AND THE DRAMA

Browning: Selections. Lyrical and dramatic poems. With the essay on Browning from E. C. STEDMAN'S " Victorian Poets." Edited by EDWARD T. MASON. 257 pp. 60 cents.

Byron: Selections. Edited, with introduction and notes, by F. I. CARPENTER, Assistant Professor in the University of Chicago. lviii+412 pp. $1.00.

Ford: The Broken Heart. With introduction and notes by CLINTON SCOLLARD, sometime Professor in Hamilton College. xvi+132 pp. 60 cents.

Lyly: Endymion. With introduction and notes by GEORGE P. BAKER, Professor in Harvard University. cxxvi+109 pp. 85 cents.

Marlowe: Edward II. And selections from TAMBURLAINE THE GREAT, and the POEMS. With notes and an introductory essay by EDWARD T. McLAUGHLIN, Professor in Yale University. xxi+120 pp. 60 cents.

Milton: Minor English Poems. With an introduction and notes by MARTIN W. SAMPSON, Professor in Cornell University. li+345 pp. 60 cents.

Pope: Selections. Edited by EDWARD B. REED, Ph.D., Assistant Professor in Yale University. xxx+241 pp. 75 cents.

Shakespeare: Merchant of Venice. Edited by THOMAS M. PARROTT, Professor in Princeton University. xli+220 pp. 35 cents.

Tennyson: The Princess. Edited, with notes, introduction, and analytical questions, by L. A. SHERMAN, Professor in the University of Nebraska. lxi+185 pp. 35 cents.

HENRY HOLT & CO. 34 West 33d Street, New York
378 Wabash Avenue, Chicago

Pancoast's Introduction to English Literature

By HENRY S. PANCOAST. *Third Edition, Revised and Enlarged.* ix + 656 pp. 12mo. $1.35.

This edition has been entirely rewritten and printed from new plates on a larger page. Greater space has been given to the Early and the Middle English periods and to the literature of the Queen Anne and Victorian periods. Lives of Bunyan, Dryden, Steele, Cowper, and others have been added.

C. G. CHILD, *Professor in the University of Pennsylvania:*—It is far and away the best elementary text-book of English Literature in existence.

WILLIAM LYON PHELPS, *Professor in Yale University:*—This is an exceedingly valuable book, in fact one of the best summaries of English Literature that has ever been written.

JAMES HUGH MOFFATT, *Central High School, Philadelphia, Pa.:*—I have always liked this book because it shows so clearly that English Literature is an expression of national life, and because it is not only about literature but is literature itself.

DR. ALBERT LEONARD, *Superintendent of Schools, New Rochelle, N. Y.:*—The book has been made even better than it was before the revision. There is no better text-book for High School work in English Literature than this book, and I am sure that this revised edition will win a still larger number of friends.

Pancoast's Introduction to American Literature

By HENRY S. PANCOAST. xii + 393 pp. 16mo. $1.12.

THE NATION:—Quite the best brief manual of the subject we know. . . . National traits are well brought out without neglecting organic connections with the mother country. Forces and movements are as well handled as personalities, the influence of writers hardly less than their individuality.

HENRY HOLT AND COMPANY

NEW YORK   CHICAGO

www.ingramcontent.com/pod-product-compliance
Lightning Source LLC
Chambersburg PA
CBHW030105030726
47498CB00007B/2262